MW01241151

DEATH
BY
ARRANGEMENT

KATHLEEN TORIAN TAYLOR

JGKS
Press
the past comes to life

www.jgkspressmystrikingly.com
5500 E. Brook Way, Elk Grove CA 95758

Publisher's Cataloging-in-Publication Data
provided by Five Rainbows Cataloging Services

Names: Taylor, Kathleen Torian, author.
Title: Death by arrangement / Kathleen Torian Taylor.
Description: Elk Grove, CA : JGKS Press, 2021.
Identifiers: ISBN 978-1-73584-270-7 (paperback) | Also available in ebook format.
Subjects: LCSH: Murder--Fiction. | Serial murderers--Fiction. | Kidnapping--Fiction. | San Francisco (Calif.)--Fiction. | Romance fiction. | BISAC: FICTION / Romance / Suspense. | FICTION / Mystery & Detective / Women Sleuths. | GSAFD: Love stories. | Suspense fiction. | Mystery fiction.
Classification: LCC PS3620.A95 D43 2021 (print) | LCC PS3620.A95 (ebook) | DDC 813/.6--dc23.

Cover design by Karen Phillips at Phillips Covers
Book design by Maureen Cutajar at Go Published

To my mom, Rose Marie Torian.
You have walked by my side with your
love and support all my life.

CHAPTER 1

June 2014
Lake Malibu

He let the car roll down the hill and listened to the dry crunch of branches under the tires. The car slowed into a large grove of trees far away from the camping area. At 11:00 p.m. Lake Malibu lit up with the full moon's silver reflections. He pressed the window button and the glass slid down. After he turned off the engine, the cool air and the aroma of pine jumpstarted his energy as it always had.

He fingered the knife in his pocket and took in the scattered picnic tables and pines. There was the perfect tree by the lake. He used to play a game there, dividing the space between soldiers, good and bad. He'd stand on the good table, holding a sword he made from a branch and yell his command, "Surrender, or die!" Since Mother was his only audience, she'd cheer as he won the battle.

He scanned the view of the water and what was once their vacation home cradled within the Santa Monica Mountains. *Mother, remember the ghost story about the Lady of the Lake? I was sure she would drag me out of bed and plunge me into her dark world. And the old movies they'd show at night, Mother, so many of them* — How Green Was My Valley, Mr. Blandings Builds His Dream House. *We'd devour a box of chocolate-covered cherries.*

A branch crackled and he grabbed his chest. A deer paused in front of the car. Only a doe. They shared a quiet moment, and then she evaporated into the brush.

He wrapped his hands around the leather steering wheel and lowered his forehead onto its forgiving softness. He could smell those hamburgers sizzling on an old black cast iron pan as he and Mother huddled together by the campfire. They melted chocolate bars and marshmallows crushed between graham crackers. She applied white cream on his nose so it wouldn't burn. They'd drift for hours in their paddleboat. The wind would lift her dark, shoulder-length hair. She always had a sheer red scarf tied around her neck. Her signature piece of clothing, along with her cardigan sweater and pleated skirt. Mother had deep brown eyes that spoke to you without words.

Enough of walking through the past. He popped open the glove compartment and took out a plastic bag filled with chopped heads of lavender. He gathered a few and squeezed them between his fingers. Mother's scent issued forth and filled the air. He retrieved the small box of chocolate-covered cherries, Mother's favorite, and tucked it along with the lavender into his jacket pocket.

Time to finish up. As he rubbed his hands together, adrenaline surged through him with the force of a waterfall. He looked over his shoulder to make sure no campers had come up behind him. After releasing the trunk, he stepped out of the car. In the distance a dog barked — he ducked. The sound drifted into silence.

After digging into his coat pocket, he removed a pair of latex gloves, tugged them onto his hands, and snapped them at the wrists. What a long day. Things needed to be tidied up. He made one last inspection to make sure no late-night campers were out for an evening jaunt, then headed for the rear of the car. The trunk stood halfway open. His hand slid along the cold metal. He pushed the lid and it drifted up, revealing its contents.

He gazed down at her. She was dressed in a pleated skirt and cardigan sweater. *There you are, my latest triumph. You look as if you decided to curl up and take a nap.* He laughed a little at the duct tape across her mouth. *You no longer need that, do you?*

He ducked his head under the lid. *You're staring up at me.* He closed her eyelids and noted rigor mortis had not yet set in. Her skin had turned an ashen color. He peeled the tape off her mouth, then took the knife from his jacket pocket and cut the rope binding her hands and ankles.

You're so petite — probably don't weigh more than a hundred pounds. Removing her from the trunk was not as easy as he'd imagined. Her body was already stiffening.

He concentrated on the lake and spotted the perfect tree. As he lowered her against its trunk, he momentarily lost his balance. She slipped through his fingers like some discarded bag of trash. *I'm sorry, Theresa. Mother always scolded me for being so awkward.* Her skirt rode up her thighs. Pinching his lips and swearing under his breath, he nudged her until she was positioned against the coarse bark. When he heard a twig snap, he fell to his side. Only a squirrel. He watched it dart up a tree, and his nerves electrified. *Hurry up.*

Time to get his arrangements underway. He always dressed his girls in the proper attire, and he was especially proud of this one. He stretched out her legs and removed the shoes. They would be added to his collection. He crossed her ankles and folded her hands across her lap. He made sure the pleated skirt covered her knees, and he buttoned the top of her cardigan sweater.

Theresa, I told you the evening would be exciting. If only I had someone to share my latest accomplishment with. Someone who'd appreciate the effort that goes into my creative process.

After removing a comb from his pocket, he parted her hair down the middle, then flicked away a few pine needles that drifted onto her arm. Her soft brown waves touched her shoulders. Pulling back her bangs to the right, he clipped on a tortoise-shell barrette to complete the look. He applied deep red lipstick to her lips, retrieved a red sheer scarf from his pants pocket, smoothed out its wrinkles, and tied the scarf around her neck.

There, that hides those nasty bruises. Kneeling beside her, he turned to face the lake. *You have a perfect view. I wish we could've spent more time talking about your art exhibit. Not the greatest, but your work probably attracted tourists.* He took one last look at the lake and then back at her. There was such purity about her posed against the tree.

Have to leave now. He ran his hand down one side of her hair, smoothing a couple of uncooperative strands. *Goodbye.* He slid the chocolates from his jacket pocket and placed the box on her lap. After removing the plastic bag of lavender, he rubbed the purple heads behind her ears and the soft veins of her wrists.

He rose and took another look to make sure no one was heading his way. *Must be almost midnight.*

He ambled back to the car, kicking small pinecones out of his path. Just another guy out for a stroll. Glancing down he noticed a thin layer of dust on his new Italian leather shoes. *Mother would not approve of dirty loafers. Hmmm. Time for a shoeshine.*

2
CHAPTER

San Francisco
November 2014

Today's predicted light rain had changed into a pinpricking slanted downpour. I popped open my umbrella. The wind seized hold, turned it inside out, and sent it flying down the street with all the other dead umbrellas. The cab rolled up in front of my apartment.

I tried several times to open the taxi's passenger door, but it seemed to be rusted shut. By the time the door decided to cooperate, my shoes were taking in water like an industrial-sized sponge. The handle finally gave way, and I slid into the back seat.

The cab smelled of stale fried chicken. Static filled the radio and I heard something about five women being murdered: "The women . . . against trees . . . cases connected . . ."

Thinking about murder was not a great way to start the evening. A shiver rippled through me. Was it from being soaked or the mention of homicide?

My two best friends thought it would be a good idea to put me back in the line of fire with a blind date. I wasn't ready to throw away another three years of my life on some asshole. I compared my last relationship with Sam to being tossed overboard, attacked by a shark that devoured large chunks of my soul.

I asked the driver, "Is it possible to find a station that doesn't sound like butter crackers being crumbled into a bowl?" I took off one of my shoes and shook drops of water onto the floorboard.

Without a word, the cabbie switched off the radio. He unwrapped a stick of gum and jammed it in his mouth. His jaw chomped up and down, and I spotted his wedding ring. Pity the poor woman when he tramps through her front door every night. Charming guy.

"Where to?" He blurted.

"Courtney's restaurant on Fell Street. Do you know it?" The rain was coming down in sheets.

"Yeah, I know it."

Fifteen minutes later, we arrived at Courtney's. The cabbie tapped the brakes — my head jerked in response. Not bothering to glance back, he struck the meter box and grumbled, "Twelve bucks."

"What? No extra charge for that smooth stop?" I presented my best sarcastic smile to the back of his head and handed him twelve bills, no tip.

I climbed out of the cab and slammed the door behind me. The rain reduced to a drizzle. I peered up at the sky. Clouds resembling black shredded scarves passed across the moon.

"Jerk!" I spat as the he took off. My sentiment dissolved unheard, down Market Street.

My throbbing veins were about to detonate. Once again, my friends had stage-managed a blind date for me. My bankrupt relationship with Sam had ended a year ago. I hadn't put my neck in the ringer since.

I removed my raincoat and gave it a hard shake. The familiar touch of Courtney's front door delivered a moment of warmth. A poster of torch singer Emma Shool was taped to the glass. I urged open the heavy wooden panel, and the sound of Emma's silky jazz replaced the roar of the wind. I tipped my head back. The door slid shut against the outside world.

I took in the scene. Tucked into one corner sat the saxophone and piano players with Emma in front. A half-dozen or so small tables and chairs surrounded the elevated platform.

I'll be on that stage someday.

The little brat inside me wanted to drag out a chair, order a martini with two toothpick-stabbed olives, and let the music swallow me. It wasn't too late to call my friends and tell them I contracted a virus that only attacked young women dumped by self-centered pricks.

No. I had to follow through with the plan. *Buck up, Sarah, it's only a few hours of angst-ridden conversation.*

The bar and restaurant were separated by two side-by-side mahogany doors, decorated with carvings of the Golden Gate Bridge. I leaned against one door and the bridge split in half. The scent of basil, rosemary, home-made soup, and freshly baked bread wafted into the air. My stomach growled. Paintings of the original Cliff House, Playland, and Laughing Sally enhanced the walls.

While I made my way through the bar crowd, my hand brushed against velvet chairs covered in rich burgundy and hunter green. White linen cloths topped the tables; a single candle warmed each center. I spotted Courtney's owner, Tom, my friend since college days. He moved his tall body through the crowd like a dancer. He had blond hair and a set of blue eyes that would catch any woman's attention. His encouragement led to my decision to make my singing debut on his stage.

Soon I'd be planting my feet where Emma stood, releasing my voice before friends and strangers. The tension in my neck increased. I wasn't sure I was ready. What if I suddenly developed a case of tone deafness and they booed me off the stage? The little voice in my head needed to shut up.

I edged farther into the crowd where lovers leaned in close, lips brushing ears with secret promises. One young couple clinked their glasses together. Were they celebrating some romantic anniversary? Sam and I had a hyper-awareness when we touched. Our toasts had promised love without end. *What a joke.* Nausea surged in me.

Time seemed to slow as I headed toward the back of the restaurant. My fingers curled and uncurled, and when I tried to force my legs to turn and run, they refused. I should never have agreed to this set up. *Dammit!*

Perspiration formed above my upper lip. My tongue snuck out and tasted the first salty drop. I dabbed off the remainder with the back of my hand. The rhinestone bracelets waving from my wrist reflected the chandelier lights, and then I caught my first glimpse of my friend Liz. Her smile showed off her white teeth. She tucked her hand under her long blond hair and finished off with a dramatic flip.

Her husband Paul raised one arm and called out my name. They had a solid marriage, but lately I'd noticed them engaging in a few more arguments, nothing major.

I switched my focus to the back of the head belonging to an extra man at their table. I didn't recognize him from the hair color—thick, black, and wavy. The lights picked up a deep shine. His face came into view—I sucked in a quick breath. Handsome was an understatement. I tugged hard on one of my earrings. *Ouch.* Maybe this small discomfort would distract me from his emerald green eyes. *Well, Sarah, no turning back now.*

3
CHAPTER

I inhaled and exhaled deeply before reaching the table of doom. Nicole and her husband Bill sat to the right of the mystery man. An empty seat separated him from Liz and Paul. That chair had to be mine.

"Hi, darlings, how's everyone doing?" My artificial voice sounded an octave higher like a distant relative of Jekyll and Hyde's.

"Darlings?" Nicole raised an eyebrow. Did anyone else appear to be confused? She was one of the most beautiful women I'd ever met. Her mother was from India and her father was Italian. Her deep-brown, exotic eyes tended to draw men's attention.

Bill stretched across and patted my arm. I was impressed by the romance between Nicole and Bill. They still held hands after ten years together.

My blind date, the black-haired Mr. Gorgeous, stood,

and to my delight, our shoulders were almost parallel. My height, five-foot-eleven, sometimes intimidated my dates. But he rose slightly above my eye level even though I was wearing stiletto heels.

He drew out the chair soon to be warmed by my clenched butt. I appraised his elevated cheekbones and olive skin. He belonged in that new men's magazine, *The Best of the Best*. He offered his hand for a shake, and it was warm and slightly calloused. "Hi. I'm Jerard Colbert." So close. The room was shrinking.

I shook his hand and again took in the color of his green eyes. His crisp blue-and-white pinstriped shirt, with its highly starched, creased sleeves, made me wonder. Did he do his own ironing or send it out to a professional?

Liz broke the awkward silence. "You going to introduce yourself, Sarah?" Like a frustrated mother, she attempted to move me along. That girl was always on a deadline.

"I'm Soon — I mean Sarah. Sorry — Sarah Soon." Great start.

Liz lowered her head and covered her mouth.

"Glad to meet you." Jerard motioned for me to take the seat.

Well, the guy had manners. That was refreshing. I slid into my chair and he returned to his. We were so packed in that his leg brushed mine. Was the heat going up a few degrees, or was I experiencing early menopause?

The name Jerard fit. He certainly wasn't Mark, my junior high school boyfriend with the coke-bottle glasses, or

Jake, my senior prom date with the powder-blue tuxedo, ruffled shirt, flood pants, and white socks.

He took a sip from his glass, and I managed a quick glimpse of his profile. Drool formed on the right side of my mouth. I peered down at my slightly bulging stomach. I was glad I decided on a loose blouse and skirt. No more late-night popcorn. *Suck it in, Sarah.* Good thing I didn't wear my business suit that buttoned up just below my chin and suggested, "Touch me, and I'll slap you from here to New York."

The waiter took my drink order. The group seemed to be halfway through their first round.

Dear Tom brought us a bottle of Cabernet.

"Hey, Tom." Nicole pointed toward the newcomer. "Jerard just moved here and your restaurant was on his list as one of the best." She beamed.

Tom uncorked the bottle of wine, eased over to Jerard, and poured him a glass. As he filled the others he said, "Welcome to San Francisco. Hope you enjoy your meal." He left the bottle in front of Jerard.

Tom extended a soft squeeze on my shoulder before disappearing back into the crowd.

Jerard moved the glass of wine to the left side of his plate and took a sip of what looked like club soda.

Maybe he didn't drink. I picked up the menu to keep my hands busy. I needed to relax and be a bit more open.

Jerard inclined toward Nicole, "Thanks for inviting me for dinner."

Nicole peeked over her menu.

Emma's singing was piped into the restaurant. Jerard tapped his fingers to the music. "I'm a big fan of jazz." He regarded me. "What would you recommend from the menu?" He moved closer and appeared to be waiting for an enthusiastic response.

Maybe he was just as nervous as I was, or maybe he didn't want to be here anymore than I did. *Just tell me you want to leave, and we can head for the front door. We'll exchange a friendly handshake and depart in different directions.*

"I think I've tried just about everything on the menu," I said, "and it's all delicious. The chef isn't afraid to experiment with various spices. Be careful, though. Ask about the heat in some of the dishes before you order." My throat felt dry.

I picked up my wine glass, sensed Jerard's eyes fixed on me, and my body temperature did a rise-and-fall act again. I pretended to study the menu that I'd already memorized.

"Sorry I'm transfixed by your hair. It's the most stunning red," Jerard said.

His attention brought on my nervous cough.

I switched my focus over to Nicole. *Help me out here, girl.*

She winked.

The waiter showed up at the right time and took our orders. Nicole restarted the conversation. "Jerard, I'm glad you could join us."

He took another sip of his drink.

I sighted a deep cut on the back of his hand holding the soda water. The wound was red with thick scar tissue. Must have happened recently. He appeared to catch me staring because he set down his glass and covered the scar with the other hand.

Spots of color coated his cheeks. "Thanks for inviting me."

Nicole sat back. "Moving to a new city can be lonely. Liz and Paul know how I met you, but I'm sure Sarah would like the details."

Jerard put his elbows on the table and tucked his right hand under his chin. "I try to visit as many art galleries as I can when I move to a new city. It gives me an idea of the culture, the heartbeat. The gallery's a perfect atmosphere for your mosaics, Nicole, and—"

Paul, Liz's husband, interrupted. "Your job relocates you often?"

"Yes," Jerard said.

"What kind of work do you do that has you moving so much?" Paul asked, his voice clipped.

Liz elbowed Paul. "Hey, would you quit interrogating Jerard, and let Nicole finish her story?"

Nicole nodded. "Patricia Torsella's gallery on Chestnut is one of my favorites. Anyway, Jerard was admiring the table I recently added to my collection. The one with colored stones, glass, and shells."

"Oh—no." Bill shook his head. "I bet you got the entire sales pitch, didn't you, Jerard?"

Nicole raised her chin. "I observed him for a while

and decided he might be a potential customer. He wandered through the gallery, but he kept returning to my work."

"She was moving in for the kill. Poor Jerard, you had no idea." Bill snickered.

Jerard massaged his cheek. "Your pitch should be written down in a sales manual. I was ready to hand you my credit card halfway through."

I stole the conversation from Nicole. "Where do you live?" Maybe the glass of wine was building up my confidence, or maybe I wanted to find out a little more about this man who loved art.

Jerard shifted toward me. "I'm leasing an apartment on Nob Hill."

Nicole cleared her throat. "He recently moved to San Francisco and needed to start shopping for furniture, along with a few pieces from local artists."

Paul crossed his arms. "Nob Hill? Nice area, expensive. Whatever your work, it must pay well." He settled back. "So, what is it that you do?"

"Will you stop?" The anger in Liz's voice surprised me. Her hands messed with her hair. "Sorry, I—oh—never mind. Nicole, maybe you can finish your story without any more interruptions from *him*." She wagged a thumb at Paul.

"Hey, honey, I'm just adding to the conversation. You don't mind questions, do you Jerard?"

"No." *That was it, just—no.*

The rest of us went silent. Four sets of eyes traveled back and forth between the wrestlers in the match. I would have to call Liz this week. Something was going on between her and Paul. What had put him in this interrogation mode?

4
CHAPTER

A moment later I tossed in my thoughts. "Jerard, I'm sorry. Paul's a little overprotective of me since I've gotten out of a bad, three-year relationship. The guy broke my heart in thirty-two pieces, and Paul's doing his best to put Miss Humpty Dumpty back together again."

"Sorry to hear that. How's Miss Dumpty doing now?" Jerard tried a bit of humor.

I said, "She's got a few cracks, but she's on the mend." There was hope. He made me feel free, not so tightly bound.

Nicole's lips drew into two straight lines. Was she annoyed by the interruptions?

She continued, "Anyway, Jerard was thinking about adding some color to his sun porch. Of course, my table would be perfect. Imagine the morning sun picking up the mosaic colors, then having coffee there with your significant one." She stirred her arms, painting the scene.

I couldn't help myself. "Boy, you are really improving on your previous pitches." So much drama over a table. My posture stiffened. If he did have a significant other, what was he doing here? If he had someone, please tell me so I could slam down the rest of my wine and take another wretched cab ride home.

Nicole retained her focus on Jerard. "Oh, wait, you told me you lived by yourself, right?" She directed an arched brow my way.

I stole a sidelong glance at him, trying my best to see his reaction.

The edge of his mouth curved up. "Yes, I live alone." He dabbed his forehead with a napkin. "Nicole told me if I didn't purchase the table, her cat would starve, her husband would go without a birthday present, and her mother's yearly dues for her Native Daughters group would go unpaid. And she wouldn't be able to have Liz read her tarot cards for two weeks."

He was funny. I needed to relax, unclench the tight cheeks of my derriere, and allow my popcorn belly to breathe.

Bill threw Nicole a dagger-like scowl. "God, it's not like we're poor. You need to change your sales pitch. This is embarrassing."

"I know, honey, but I did sell the table." She straightened the collar of her blouse. "Jerard, when I first met Nicole, she talked me into buying a mosaic of dancing ants. It's in a closet somewhere. I can't seem to part with the thing." Bill shook his head, took in a deep breath, and exhaled.

"Dancing ants?" Jerard held his fist against his lips. "How much did she charge you?"

"One hundred dollars plus tax. She also convinced me to take her to dinner." Bill's face softened; maybe he was remembering their first meeting.

I tucked my hair behind an ear. What was it like to have a marriage like theirs? They had fun teasing each other—it was part of their relationship. They'd been married for ten years, just like Paul and Liz. How did they make it work? Would I have it someday?

"Are you an artist?" Jerard asked.

Bill chuckled. "One artist is enough in our household. I teach history at Balboa High School."

"We're a true example of opposites attract." Nicole snaked an arm around Bill's shoulder.

Everyone snickered except for Paul. He continued to lean back in his chair, and his focus narrowed on Jerard.

"How many times have you moved?" Paul used his full detective voice.

Jerard's jaw tightened. "Maybe eight or nine."

Did Paul see something in Jerard that I needed to be aware of?

"Must get old after a while." Paul did not shift his concentration.

Jerard shrugged his shoulders.

I picked up my spoon and twirled it between my fingers. *Lighten up, Paul. Do you think he's a womanizer or did you see him in one of your lineups?*

5
CHAPTER

I squinted down at my watch. An hour had passed since my arrival. "Where's our food? I'm starving." In the next instant, I saw the waiter heading our way — *finally*.

I'd ordered broiled chicken breast with a blend of basil and rosemary. I sank my fork into Courtney's famous twice-baked potato. The center separated, spilling melted Gorgonzola cheese over the sides. Crumbled bacon bits topped it off. I decided to skip dessert.

Tom stopped by our table again. "How's everything here?"

The group grinned through mouthfuls of food.

He whispered. "I see you ordered your favorite, Sarah."

I nodded, assuming the impression of a squirrel with nuts stored in both cheeks.

"Enjoy." Tom disappeared into the crowd.

Jerard acknowledged the food on his plate. "Looks a lot better than my salad. I should lighten up on healthy choices." He sniffed the aroma of cheese and bacon, then shook out his white cloth napkin and draped it over his lap.

Nice manners. I'd like to meet his mother. She did a good job. I looked over at his healthy chef salad, dressing on the side, no croutons, and another club soda. Was he questioning the cheesy potato mounted on my fork making a hasty journey to my mouth? *I promise, Jerard, once we're married, I'll cut back on the carbs.*

Paul forked his mashed potatoes into a miniature volcano. "Jerard, where'd you live before you moved here?"

Here we go again. I took a sip of wine and observed the two men engaging in this little game. What were they up to?

Jerard took his time before answering. He swallowed a bite of salad, then dabbed the corner of his mouth with his napkin. "Los Angeles for a few months; before that, New York. I troubleshoot for small art galleries with financial problems, so I go where the work is." He picked up his fork and impaled another leaf.

"Who are you working for in San Francisco?" Paul fiddled with his food.

"Oh, for heaven's sake," Nicole snapped. She dug into her handbag and removed a small card. "Here's Jerard's business card with his first and last names—even has a phone number." Jerard observed Paul for an uncomfortable few seconds. "I have several art galleries in the Oakland and Half Moon Bay areas that I'm working with. I've always wanted to live in San Francisco, so I took the jobs. It doesn't take up much of my time, and I'm getting to know the city."

"Did you say your last name was Colbert?" Paul rubbed his left index finger back and forth across his chin. He picked up the card and turned it over. "You spell your first name different than normal."

I tapped a finger against the stem of my wine glass. What? Did Paul think the man didn't know how to spell his own name? *Jeez, give him a break.*

"Yes, I spell my name differently." Jerard's tone hardened.

"And Colbert — that's Irish isn't it?"

"Yes," Jerard said.

I propped my chin with my hand. "Are you having fun yet, he who spells his name differently?" I produced a tacky grin. "The food you have to pay for, but the interrogation is free."

"Good to know." His voice relaxed, but not much.

Bill, Liz, and Nicole seemed as confused as I was. A lot of head turning and elbow nudging were underway.

"All right, Paul. Satisfied? Do you think you could stop being a cop for one night?" Liz shoved his shoulder.

"You're a cop?" Jerard adjusted himself.

"I recently made detective," Paul said.

"Guess you're curious. It's okay — I don't mind the questions." Jerard's fork made a sharp sound as it dropped onto his salad plate. "You want to make sure Sarah's not spending the evening with some psychopath."

I smirked. Sam, the cheater, to Jerard, the psycho-path—that would be a leap.

"You're not one, are you?" Paul asked.

Liz's palm ground into the table "Sorry, Jerard. Mr. Cop here doesn't seem to be able to leave his badge at home." She shot Paul the stare that initiated their every fight.

Paul dropped the conversation and took a large bite of hamburger. He continued stuffing his face.

Was the drilling session over?

A flash of light from Jerard's wristwatch returned my attention to the scar on his left hand. The cut was in full view while he drained his glass. The scar stretched from his wrist to his index finger. The stitches were gone, yet the wound remained red and swollen.

I edged forward for a better view. "What happened to your hand?" I realized I was squinting, so I rested back in my chair.

"Last date didn't like my politics." He shrugged.

"Good one," Bill said as Nicole joined the amuse-ment.

I pressed my lips together. I didn't think it was that funny. How did he get the cut? A fight? An accident?

"Nasty cut. Knife?" Paul asked.

"Yeah, but it's healing pretty well." Jerard dropped his hand in his lap.

My nervous cough returned.

Jerard bent toward me. "You okay? Here, take a sip." He handed me my water glass.

The sip soothed my throat, but not the mistrust

dancing in my brain. Tired of the banter, I needed a break. "Excuse me." I scooted my chair back and fled to the restroom.

6
CHAPTER

I dodged a few waiters with large trays of food and used my hip to shove open the women's door. Quiet at last. Restrooms could be lifesavers sometimes. This evening was like having a dental checkup—painful and not covered by insurance. What was up with Paul and Jerard?

The lavatory included a small powder room complete with a sofa. To my mind, the couch was provided for those suffering from blind-date syndrome. I dropped onto the cushions. *Relax.* We'd wrap up with some polite goodbyes and go home

A few minutes later the door opened, bringing in a cool breeze and the din of the restaurant crowd, along with Nicole and Liz, their foreheads etched with concern.

Liz sat next to me and took my hand. "You could use a bit of blush on that pale face of yours."

"What can we do to bring you back to Mr. Green Eyes?" Nicole plopped down on an arm of the couch.

"Well, for starters you should have never arranged this date. What were you thinking?" My words sounded loud, choppy. "Sorry. I needed a few moments alone. I'll be okay. This date thing was a mistake. I should have had the courage to say no, but you two seem to think I need to be with some guy to make me whole again. Besides, why all these questions from Paul?"

"You know Paul—once a cop, always a cop." Liz slapped my thigh gently.

"I know you mean well, but maybe I'm not ready for this." My elbows rested on my knees.

Nicole slipped off the sofa arm and sat by my other side. "It's been over a year now since Sam. Get over it. Move on."

"I don't transition at your allocated speed." I shoved off the sofa and paced for a few seconds. "You've got everything mapped out for me, don't you?"

Nicole said, "It's just that you seem to be stuck in the Sam hellhole. It's time you nudge open the door to your heart and let someone say hello again." Her way with words calmed me down.

I stopped pacing and faced them; I struck my upper left chest. "It's going to take a locksmith to even begin to unseal this heart. Thanks for coming to check on me. One more minute and I might have tried to escape from that two-by-four window. Of course, I'd get stuck and you'd have to call the fire department. I guess returning to the table might be a better idea." I stepped over to the sink, splashed some water on my face, and dried it with a towel.

Nicole put her hands on the back of my shoulders and spun me around to face her. "What *do* you think of Jerard?"

"He's gorgeous. Seems nice. Not sure I have an opinion formed yet. I need to go slow, so you two need to give me some time. Okay?"

They crossed their hearts and faked a Girl Scout salute.

"I guess it's true what they say about women's restrooms," I quipped.

"What do they say?" Liz checked herself in the mirror, took out her lipstick, and applied a fresh coat.

"When one woman heads to the restroom, all the others join her."

They wrapped their arms around me, let go, and Liz held the door. "Come on, gals, it's time to mosey back to our men folk." She executed her best Southern accent.

"Our men folk? Well then, let's hitch up and get along." Nicole tugged up her pants and bowed her legs like a bull rider.

It was now almost nine o'clock. When we returned to the table, Jerard rose and gripped the chair, signaling me to sit. Liz and Nicole admired his deed and pressed their husbands to do the same. Bill made a grand gesture by bowing after Nicole was seated.

Paul didn't get up. Liz glared and he said, "What?"

The waiter cleared the table and brought us coffee. To my surprise, Jerard ordered Courtney's famous peach cobbler with a scoop of vanilla ice cream.

I breathed in the aroma of warm peaches, recalling the taste of a crust that screamed "a cup of butter," and then I glanced at Jerard.

"I always save the best for last. I'm a sucker for sweets." His smile resembled a Cheshire cat's.

He was human after all. I had an urge to pick up my spoon and invade his territory of sweet things. Instead I picked up my cup of boring decaf.

Liz clinked her knife against her cup. "I think it's time to bring up our monthly challenge." She flicked her long blonde hair off her shoulders. "Jerard, once a month we get together and do something out of our comfort zone. I came up with this idea because Paul and I needed adventure. We were spending too much time watching reality TV."

Paul did a little eye roll. "And, of course, I went along with her."

Liz repeated the gesture with her big blues. "Anyway, I recruited the rest of our group to join us. This month I've signed us up for a dance class."

Paul rubbed a hand over his short-cropped hair.

Jerard scraped the last few pieces of crust from his plate, laid down his fork, and gave his attention to Liz.

Was he excited about this idea? I certainly was not.

Liz continued. "We'll meet at the Let's Dance Studio on the corner of Mission and 24th, six o'clock tomorrow."

"What kind of dance class?" I asked. I didn't like the idea of making a fool of myself.

"West Coast Swing." She raised her shoulders up and down in a little jig.

I squeezed my shoulder blades together. The blind date wasn't enough to deal with? Now they had me participating in some kind of dance class?

"I'm not sure our group is ready to become swingers." Nicole's forehead crease could hold a quarter.

Liz clasped her hands as if she were giving the Sermon on the Mount. "Come on, girls. This gives us a chance to dig out that sassy little dress engulfed in the back of our closets. Wear comfortable shoes. Please, no running shoes, maybe something with a low heel."

Liz and Nicole agreed with a slight nod.

I'd decide later.

Liz said, "It would be nice if we gals could find a dress that has a little flare at the bottom and men, if you have a pair of suspenders, that would add a bit of 1940s style. Actually, some men in the Forties wore what was called a Zoot suit, but I think that would be going a little too far for our guys." She shrugged.

Paul stirred. He rested his arm around the back of Liz's chair. "Honey, are you sure there isn't something else we could try? How's this for an idea? I could take everyone to the shooting range, you know, the one on Third Street, and teach them how to use a gun. No dancing, just point and shoot. What do you think?" He flexed his eyebrows a few times, trying to do his best impression of Groucho Marx. All he needed was a cigar.

Liz huffed. "Paul, you know the thought of a weapon makes me nervous. I don't think our friends would enjoy an evening of blasting holes in the outline of someone's head."

"Yeah, but it'd shove you out of your comfort zone." He applied a small kiss to her cheek.

"Hey." I clapped my hands. "I'm all for it. I'd rather shoot at something than put a heel through my dance partner's shoe."

Liz narrowed her eyes at Paul.

"Okay, West Coast Swing it is." Paul raised his hands in surrender.

"I took some ballroom dancing in college." Jerard's voice sounded eager. "I wouldn't mind taking a class. I'm not too bad at dancing. I even have a few ribbons from a couple of contests. I'm willing if you are, Sarah." He flashed his emerald eyes, and my toes wiggled inside my fire-engine red stilettos.

I tugged my fingers through my Irish red, tightly curled hair, settling the mayhem in my stomach.

Jerard cupped my other hand.

Did his touch suggest I calm down or was he trying to let me know how exciting this adventure would be? *Breathe, Sarah.* "Sure, I'm willing to get out there and make a fool of myself with the rest of my crazy friends." I threw up my hands up and surrendered like Paul had to his Queen Liz.

Nicole rotated her wedding ring. "Is this a beginner's class or do we need some kind of experience?"

Bill tugged on his beard while Paul nibbled his thumbnail and eyed Jerard.

"Maybe a better idea would be to pick a less stressful

monthly challenge." Nicole kneaded her neck as if it were bread dough.

Liz retrieved her purse from the back of her chair. "I'm way ahead of you. I have DVDs for everyone." Her arm disappeared inside her bag, and she presented a stack of plastic cases.

I marveled at her. My friend was a true Virgo, Goddess of Organizational Skills.

"Liz, what do you do for a living?" Jerard asked.

"I work part time for the San Francisco Children's Home and volunteer at their fundraisers."

"Well, I'm astonished by your managerial abilities." Jerard brushed his hands together.

Liz squeezed the DVD cases into a perfect square pile. "Thank you." She picked up one of the DVDs and pointed at the title, *How to Learn the West Coast Swing in One Short Hour*. "I'd suggest you memorize the basic steps." She handed a copy to each one of us uncertain students.

Great, there went a relaxing Sunday. I took a quick scan of the group's reaction.

Bill over stirred his coffee, Nicole jiggled the ice cubes in her water glass, and Paul texted, something I'd never seen him do. Every so often he paused, long enough to examine Jerard.

Liz's lips shriveled like a pair of prunes, and she told him to get off the phone. He slid it under the edge of his saucer.

"The DVD will be helpful. This'll be fun," Liz said. "Remember, six o'clock, Let's Dance Studio."

I plucked a pen out of my purse and wrote the address on the back of my DVD.

The energy at the table dropped from ten to three. Next month would be my turn to pick an out-of-your-comfort-zone idea. *Guess what I'm going to choose, Liz? Sit on the couch and watch mindless TV.*

Paul's phone vibrated from under his saucer. He checked the caller's number. "Sorry, hon. It's work. I have to take this." He launched his chair back and it scraped the floor like fingernails across a chalkboard. He headed for the entrance, glancing back twice while involved in a conversation.

Knowing Paul, he was probably already doing a background check on Jerard. Since my breakup with Sam, he protected me as if I were someone attending their first day of kindergarten. I would have to chat with him about his big brother behavior. What was he up to, and what did he see in Jerard that I did not?

7
CHAPTER

The check came after we finished our coffee around ten o'clock. "Dinner's on me," Jerard announced. "It's difficult meeting people when you move to a new city."

"Very generous of you." I didn't argue about the bill. It had to be a couple hundred dollars. If nothing else, I got a free meal.

He stood up next to me and I took another glimpse of his perfectly ironed slacks. He wore a pair of deep-brown Italian loafers, so polished the light bounced off their sheen. His skin looked lightly brushed by the sun.

Jerard took my elbow and guided me through the crowd. As we gathered outside, I welcomed the cool damp air on my face. The rain stopped but the wind whipped up a pile of garbage on the street. A plastic bag wrapped around the bottom of a parking meter as if holding on for dear life.

I spotted Paul standing close to the curb. Liz strolled over and said something that did not please him, judging by the grimace on his face. Irritated, he shoved the phone into his jacket pocket. Though he took hold of Liz's arm, she shook him away with such force, for a moment he lost his balance.

Bill and Jerard enjoyed what seemed to be a lively conversation. Their shoulders bounced up and down while they shared something humorous.

Nicole appeared at my right and whispered, "Jerard. Not too bad for a blind date."

I poked her gently. "You did a pretty good job. I haven't had this much fun in a long time. If we could have vetoed the dance class, it would have been a perfect evening. I appreciate the effort you put into this plan."

She wrapped her arm around me. "You know you love your artistic, off-the-chart friend." She reunited with Bill and slid her hand into his.

Would I have this kind of intimacy someday? I missed the touch of a man's skin stirring up that hummingbird feeling.

Bill double tapped Jerard's back. "I'm glad you're going to join our dance troupe tomorrow night. We can use all the male support available. If you want to run away as far and as fast as you can, Paul and I would understand, but it might be fun."

Liz and Paul headed back to our group. As Liz stepped ahead of Paul, she seemed determined to show who won the fight. Maybe their disagreement would continue when they got home. Liz had been quick-tempered lately. This wasn't like her. I would have to give her a call and find out what was going on.

Paul extended his hand to shake Jerard's. "Good meeting you."

Jerard put out his right hand. He swept a strand of wind-blown hair with his left.

Paul examined the scar. "Man, that had to hurt!"

Jerard shoved the hand into his pants pocket. "No, pain's gone. Looking forward to tomorrow night." His tone was cool.

Liz rendered a quick peck on my cheek. "I think Nicole found the perfect blind date, don't you?"

"We'll see. Jury's still out, at least on my side, but I'll try and be more open-minded." I circled my arms around her for a brief hug. "You and Paul okay?"

"It's nothing. Just been on edge lately. Everything's bothering me. Must be hormones, I don't know."

My two best friends had been watching over me since my breakup with Sam. I needed to make time for Liz; maybe a cup of coffee together would help her vent.

Our group began to disband, and we headed to the curb to hail cabs.

"I have a town car. If you don't mind cramming four in the back seat, my driver could take all of us." Jerard signaled to a car parked across the street.

Nicole did not hesitate. "No, the four of us live out by Golden Gate Park. Sarah's place is more in your direction, over on Dolores Street." She elbowed my side and whispered, "Here's your chance. Try and give yourself some happiness again. You deserve it, friend. It's been too long."

I shoved my hands down so hard in my coat pockets that I tore the lining. Nicole and Liz set up this date, and now they were encouraging me to get in a car with a man I met only a few hours ago. On the other hand, this could turn into something more than one blind date.

Jerard touched my shoulder. "Drive you home?"

"Sure." Maybe I could find out something else about him on the way. I approached the town car. Jerard's hand rested on my upper back. His contact drove the thermostat in my body up to warm. What was it about his touch?

Paul cried out, "Hey you two!" He held up his cell-phone. "Smile." After he snapped the photo, Jerard's grin vanished.

Liz ripped the phone out of Paul's hand and crammed it into her purse. "What the hell are you doing?"

Her voice echoed in my ears. Oh, there was going to be some yelling at their house tonight. I had better call her sooner than later. Why was Liz so upset? I had never seen them like this. Embarrassed by Paul's behavior, I knew my face took on a shade of red.

Even with the fog edging in, a drop of perspiration poised on my upper lip, and I caught it with the back of my hand. I lowered my head and shut my eyes. With the way Paul was behaving, should I risk getting into a car with Jerard, a man I barely knew?

If I didn't feel comfortable after the ride home, I could always back out of the dance class. *Stop second-guessing all the time. Remember what your therapist said? "Time to take a chance and go forward."*

But Paul's behavior tugged at me like a dog with a bone.

A minute later Jerard's town car edged to a slow stop in front of us. I admired these black, shiny cars and always wondered who was behind the tinted windows. The driver beckoned us to enter the back seat. Taller than Jerard, the chauffeur's muscles stretched the fabric of his suit jacket. There was a sadness in his eyes and a hesitation in his smile. "Good evening, Ma'am." He took a step back.

"Hello," I said. Should I introduce myself to him? This was an entirely different world for me. Jerard must have made a sizable annual salary. There I was, being driven home in a town car by a personal driver, and if I remembered correctly, Jerard leased an apartment on Nob Hill. He must have done quite well troubleshooting for art galleries.

"Please, Sarah, slide on in." Jerard's breath warmed the back of my ear. The scent of the leather seats hit me right away.

Jerard put his hand on my lower spine and guided me into the car. His touch sent a thrill that turned on my internal heater. What would it be like to get closer to his skin and inhale his captivating fragrance of citrus and sandalwood? Might be a nice scent to wake up to on my pillowcase. *Okay, girl, let's reduce the speed from sex to a friendly handshake at the end of the evening.*

43

"This is certainly a step up from the cab ride over to the restaurant," I said. "That taxi smelled like dried, cracked leather and reeked of cheap perfume and day-old sandwiches. Here I feel like Cinderella." I rambled on. My usual anxiety started up. Any moment this car would turn into a pumpkin. I would run away, and Jerard would find one of my size-ten heels in the gutter.

He slid closer and his leg touched mine. Ooh, the warmth of his body. My mind started to wander again. When was the last time I wanted to be caressed by a man? My stomach tumbled like clothes in a dryer.

"What's your address?" Jerard asked.

"2120 Dolores Street." I brushed imaginary lint off my skirt. What could we possibly have in common? He was Nob Hill, had a personal driver, and might even have a chef. I decorated my apartment with second-hand furniture, took the bus to work, and the closest thing to having a chef was when I stuck a frozen dinner in the microwave.

Jerard bent forward and placed his hand on the driver's shoulder. "Joe, you know the area where Sarah lives?"

"Yes, sir." Joe's baritone voice sounded husky.

My gaze went from the back of Joe's head to the rear-view mirror. His attention held mine as he gave a quick nod. Jerard hit a button and a window divided us from the hired help. So much for introducing myself. Maybe those were the rules of the town-car set. I had no idea.

As we drew away from the curb onto Market Street, Jerard eased back in the seat. His hip caught the edge of my skirt, which slid up my thigh. All this light touching and lifting of skirts elevated my fantasies. The thought of sex with him was right up there with bagels and cream cheese on Sunday morning.

Halfway into the fifteen-minute drive, I stretched across Jerard to point out a few of my favorite neighborhood landmarks. "That's Mission Dolores Park where I spend some afternoons with my dogs. If you haven't visited Mission Dolores, put it on your list. It dates to the 1830s, and it's the oldest building in San Francisco. The cemetery has some of the most interesting people buried there. It's the final resting place of 5,000 Ohlone and Miwok Indians and other first Californians who built the mission. The Committee of Vigilance members are buried there, along with convicted murderers Cora, Casey, and Sullivan."

"I haven't been there yet."

A strand of hair fell from behind my ear. He caught it and tucked it back in place. I settled against the soft leather seat.

His head tilted toward me. "Maybe you can give me a guided tour."

"Sure." Nothing like walking through a cemetery to add some romance.

The streetlights illuminated the red gum trees that bloomed in scarlet, pink, and orange. Sam and I always loved strolling through the Mission neighborhood. I tapped the car window on my side. "The Mission area has strict rules on keeping the historical authenticity of those beautiful Victorian homes called Painted Ladies." My voice sounded higher than normal like a professional travel guide.

Jerard's upper body angled across mine, taking in the landscape through my window. His cheek showed the promise of stubble. I had a strong temptation to nibble on his earlobe. Long-forgotten feelings meandered through my memory. I'd like to give another relationship a try, but the memory of Sam pulled my emergency brake every time.

Jerard's shoulder connected with mine. "I enjoyed meeting your friends." His deep voice called me back to emerald green eyes that matched my own. They sparkled like jewels in a pirate chest.

"My girlfriends are quite the team. They both love their jobs. I have a boring job working in an accountant's office downtown. The girls are always trying to prod me outside my mold."

"You're definitely not conventional." His hand grazed my thigh and to my surprise, he left his hand there. My body felt like a slice of butter melting down the side of a warm pancake.

"Have you lived in San Francisco all your life?" he asked.

"Most of it. I relocated from Ashland, Oregon to San Francisco. I lived there with my aunt and her husband after my parents died. When I was twelve my mom passed away from cancer, and my dad had a massive heart attack. It's been fifteen years since I lost them. I thought I'd never make it through the grief, but my aunt and uncle managed to help me survive.

"Later, I experienced the loss of my uncle who died because he smoked a pack of cigarettes every day, and my aunt died seven years ago from breast cancer." I was reliving the loss along with him and the sorrow was seeping back in.

I changed the subject. "What about you? Where are you from originally?" I tossed the conversation back to his side of the net.

He hesitated before he answered, his eyes searching mine. "I started out back East and — "

The car slowed and he didn't finish his answer.

"This is it." I pointed to the royal-blue Victorian, its exterior a mix of plum, purple, and cream. "It's been converted into apartments like so many of these beautiful Painted Ladies."

Joe parked. He reappeared at our door with such a forlorn face, I wanted to say, "It'll be okay." Maybe he didn't like his job.

Jerard offered his right hand to help me from the car. As I went up the front stairs, he followed. When Sam wasn't spending the night, he'd usually drop me off at the sidewalk. Sam could learn a few things from Jerard.

I sniffed the fragrance of the potted lavender and roses that lined the stairs. We stopped in front of the lobby doors. Should I invite him up for coffee? It had been a long time since I had to make this kind of decision. This was ridiculous—why couldn't I relax?

I rummaged through my purse for my keys.

Jerard placed his hands on my shoulders and lured me close to his chest. He lifted my chin and his soft lips lingered on my cheek. I could feel his warm breath. *Continue to my lips, please.* I wanted to taste his kiss.

My eyes closed; I sensed him backing up.

"Keys?"

My eyelids parted.

Crinkles appeared around the edges of his eyes, along with a faint smile.

"Oh, yes." My hands fumbled inside my purse, trying to shake off the vision of him lowering me into bed, ripping off my flannel pajamas, and having his way with me. I handed him the jingly chain holding the keys and passed it to him. Jerard wrapped his hands around the metal doorknob and unlocked the door.

My attention turned to Joe while I waited. He rested against the car, his arms crossed. The corners of his mouth curled up as if the unfolding scene amused him.

I called out, "Thanks for the ride."

He raised a hand.

Jerard said, "Tomorrow night should be fun. If it's okay with you, I'd like to pick you up at 5:30 p.m." He handed back the keys.

"Are you sure you want to put yourself through this dance project?"

He angled his head, plainly questioning my doubt.

"Yes, of course."

Did I detect a note of impatience in his voice?

He guided the door open and came so close, my face was almost buried in his chest. "Good night, Sarah." I loved the throaty way he spoke my name. I wanted to drag him upstairs, battle through two hungry dogs, and slam my bedroom door. I bit down on the inside of my lip. An X-rated movie played in my head.

I stepped into the lobby while holding onto the anti-quated doorknob. I stole one more snapshot of Jerard.

He said, "Shut the door, please. I want to make sure you're safe inside. You can never be too careful." He placed his left hand on the doorknob, flashing the scar once again.

He never did tell us how he was injured.

As I twisted the dead bolt, I heard the loud metal latch. Looking out, I watched Jerard return to the car. As Joe held the door open, he slid into the back seat. The car evaporated into traffic, carrying away the man who chipped away a few bricks from the solid wall I built over the last year.

8
CHAPTER

I waltzed over to the four metal boxes in the hallway and checked my mail. The trek up two flights took me longer than usual. My body generated a higher level of energy. My fingers glided along the bannister, and for the first time, I felt the grooves and crevices in the mahogany. How many souls touched this handcrafted support? How many couples embraced here as they fell in love?

At the door of my apartment, I heard the familiar clicking sounds of animals running across the wooden floor. I unlocked the door and gave it a shove. My two dachshunds greeted me with wagging tails and dog breath only an owner could love.

I draped my purse and coat on a hook, flipped off my shoes, and headed for the couch. My home was the two-bedroom apartment I shared with my aunt after my uncle passed away. I could still feel her presence, and every so often the fragrance of her Imperial Rose perfume visited me. A large bay window graced the front room where I spent hours watching the neighborhood wake up on Sunday mornings. Some residents would dash out in pajamas to scoop up the Sunday newspaper, hoping no one saw them.

I plopped down on the couch, its fabric now a bit age-worn, with tracks of puppies' teeth marks embedded in the cloth. I recently painted the walls in a soft peach tone that infused the room with warmth. Gracey traveled up the custom-made ramp and joined me. Max demanded hand delivery. They crawled over me like unruly children.

I retrieved the shoe that Max held in his mouth and started my one-sided dialogue. "What a night I had! Maybe I'm on the mend. I wonder if Jerard likes dogs. Don't worry, if he doesn't, he's out of here."

Max's head shifted to the right. He was trying his best to understand this foreign language.

I knuckle rubbed the top of their heads. "I imagine you understand the word 'treat.'" I caught Max before he could jump off the couch. He had back problems. I worked on getting him to use the ramp, but he refused to accept that he was considered a senior. He waited and I placed him on the floor.

I moseyed into my small kitchen and popped off the top of the ceramic canister that greeted me with the aroma of freshly ground coffee beans. I set up my coffee pot for the morning and ignored the pile of mail that waited, stacked on my table for two. The table was one of my favorite finds in a thrift shop off Fillmore Street. I sanded and stained it a deep brown. Two wrought-iron chairs set it off, one on each side.

I heard low growls behind me. "Sorry. I was distracted," I said. The dogs led me toward the much-desired treat jar, and I followed like an obedient mother. The jar was a clear glass replica of Dino the Dinosaur. I lifted the head and retrieved two home-made peanut butter cookies. The treats disappeared into two once-aggressive mouths that had mellowed over the years.

"Okay, guys, time to go outside." The dogs pulled their respective sweaters off the bench by the back door, and I slid them over their heads. I jerked open the door that always stuck in the winter. Their short legs scrambled fast down the wooden stairs. The backyard was a twenty-by-twenty-foot pad of grass and weeds. A thick blanket of San Francisco fog created a soundless, ill-omened atmosphere. The dampness invaded me, sending in shivers from head to toe.

"Do your business." The dogs sniffed and hunted for dark night critters. "Come on, house, now." I clapped my hands and they skittered up behind me. After wrestling with their sweaters, I locked both back and front doors. I swiped the mail off the table and put it on my antique roll top desk in the second bedroom office.

My claw foot bathtub called to me. Though a hot bath filled with lavender beads sounded inviting, I was too tired to go through such a ritual. Instead, I twisted my long curls up in a ponytail, washed my face, and put on my sexy flannel pajamas covered in a dachshund print. I retired my non-dancer's body to bed, along with my two pals who burrowed under my aunt's handmade quilt.

9
CHAPTER

Not long afterward, I picked up the remote off the bed stand. The Channel Seven weather report was what I needed. My mind drifted from the news broadcast to Jerard. He had touched my chin for that brief cheek kiss. Then I remembered the scar on his left hand. He joked about the cut but managed to avoid an explanation. Maybe he got into a fight with an ex-lover's husband. Or maybe he was working part time for a meatpacking company and missed his mark.

My attention returned to the TV. Photographs of five women lined up across the screen. They all had shoulder-length brown hair and appeared to be about the same age, late twenties to early thirties. Their faces were familiar. They reminded me of someone, but I couldn't figure out who. Their images disappeared and the camera centered on the reporter, James Stanfield.

"According to police, the recent murder of a young woman in Los Angeles has been linked to four other murders: two in Savannah, one in Galveston, and one in Tampa. Similarities caused the police to categorize them as the work of a serial killer. Each died of strangulation with a sheer red scarf." The hairs lifted on the nape of my neck, and my bedroom seemed to shrink.

Stanfield continued. "The killer seems to stay along coastal cities, with the last murder in Los Angeles." He pointed to a map. "The five murders seem to be linked by comparable details, especially the red scarf. The unknown suspect had a habit of killing every two years. However, the last two murders occurred only six months apart. The interval between these homicides is shortening."

I sat up and tucked my knees close to my chest. Los Angeles? Didn't Jerard say he had moved here from L.A.? What were the odds of my dating a serial killer? With my track record, there might be a chance. An unusual stillness came over me. I took a sip of water from a bottle on the nightstand. I didn't want to close my eyes to this news.

The thought of someone tightening a red scarf around my neck, squeezing the last breath out of me, caused me to drag the covers closer to my chin. I must have emitted an electric surge because Max did his belly crawl and placed his wet nose on my cheek. He sniffed around my face, checking to see if I needed assistance. "You'd guard me, wouldn't you, Max?" I gave him a quick back massage.

Ten minutes of news was all I could ingest. I switched off the TV. Enough about murdered women. Untangling myself from the dogs, I slid my feet into my slippers. Nothing wrong with checking those three dead bolts again. My aunt made the decision to install them on the front door. This was her thinking on having three locks: we'd hear the first attempt to unlock number one; during the second try we'd have time to call the police; and if the third lock was broken we'd run down the back stairs. Made sense to me.

After checking the locks, I drifted back under the covers and reviewed my evening as if it were an old movie. I knew almost nothing about Jerard, but I wanted to learn more. If only I could dive into those eyes of his and discover the man inside. Should this go further? Would I cancel tomorrow's date? There was something about him that told me to keep going, take a chance. But I tried that with Sam and look what happened.

Two large hands wrapped around my neck. I scratched him so hard, I felt something wet on my fingertips. Blood? I couldn't see his face, but he exhaled hot breath onto my skin. He reeked of liquor and cigarettes. I started coughing—I was about to die. My leg muscles tightened, and I tried to jump up and run, but a demanding elbow sent a sharp pain into my chest. He was so strong. I could feel the mattress box springs vibrate under me.

I woke up disoriented. I couldn't breathe. This vision caused me to rub my hands up and down my arms, and I tried to get my circulation going. I wanted someone to hold me and whisper, "It was just a dream," but I had only the voice in my head to calm me.

I headed for the bathroom, splashed cold water on my face, and collected my quilted, extra-warm robe off the hook. I couldn't shake the chill. I flicked the button on the coffee machine and wandered over to the bay window. The street was quiet. No one was rushing off to work. It was Sunday and I looked forward to a day of leisure. After that dream I wanted to stay in my safe cocoon.

I crawled back in bed and took a few sips of coffee. Two warm, furry creatures cuddled around my feet, buried under two blankets and the quilt. I closed my eyes as the sunrise cascaded through the blinds. I flipped over my right shoulder, faced the empty side of my bed, and ran my hand down the Egyptian cotton sheets that Sam had insisted I buy. Such fancy sheets for a single person.

Had it been a year since Sam filled the space? My mind flirted with last night's date. A vision of Jerard lying next to me came to mind. His hands were caressing my breasts, awakening my lips with his tongue, searching every curve of my body.

The conga line shuffled out from under the covers and interrupted my fantasy. This morning's only hot kisses would be laced with dog saliva. They hovered around my head, forcing me to acknowledge their presence. I pretended to sleep, but Max nuzzled my neck until I opened my eyes. Then they pounced.

I covered my head with my hands, preventing their small toenails from leaving scratches. "All right, guys, a little morning news, then food." They flopped onto their backs, ready for a tummy rub. I massaged their soft bellies and grabbed the remote off the nightstand.

Watching the Sunday morning news was one of my rituals. Announcer Linda Casillas, an enthusiastic, ninety-pounder with perfect hair, flawless makeup, and bleached white teeth, spoke about today's fair on Union Street. Her earsplitting voice numbed my mind.

I drifted away from her report and thought instead of Jerard's thick hair. How would it feel to move my fingers through it? I loved the way he slid the keys out of my hand. There were few men left who did such things, so maybe I needed to stop judging the opposite sex.

I rested my head on my pillow and had another one-sided conversation with my crew. "I think I'm ready to take a risk and see where this goes. It would be nice to have someone make love to me. How long has it been since I've stood completely naked, physically and emotionally? Time I unlock the vault to my heart and let someone enjoy the treasure." My audience rolled away from me, and I could swear they yawned at the same time. I said, "Wow, you're quite the support team."

"Good morning. This is Tracy Porter." A different reporter's voice broke in—her precise words caught my attention.

I settled back into my pillow.

Her speech was disciplined. Her hazel eyes picked up light from cameras which deepened their color. She clenched her jaw, and my own shoulders tightened.

"Authorities are alarmed at similarities between the murder of a young woman in Los Angeles and four out-of-state homicides. They are categorized as the work of the same serial killer who's been crossing state lines and is now believed to be moving up the California coast. The FBI has taken over the investigation." The reporter rubbed her left temple.

A shudder took over my body. *Jeez. Will San Francisco be next?*

Her eyebrows drew together as she continued, and her eyes teared up. "The San Francisco Police Department is warning residents of the city not to travel alone at night in isolated areas. The police ask all citizens to be cautious. If you do plan to be out late, make sure you travel with several friends and not alone."

This was not a good way to start my day. I clicked off the remote and tossed it back onto the side table.

Smoothing my hand over the head of each of my ferocious watchdogs, I glanced down the hall to my front door. Wait, hadn't I heard something about the girls being found dead next to trees? I slapped my thigh. The radio in the cab ride? Yes, that's where I heard it.

The girls were all strangled. What were their last thoughts? Did they know and trust this man? Assuming it *was* a man.

10
CHAPTER

At 9:00 a.m. I had enough depressing news and I needed fresh air. I threw on my Sunday morning sweatpants, sweatshirt, and coat. I packed my coffee thermos into a bag. The dogs lined up at the front door, their leashes and jackets in their mouths. "Drop," I commanded. They obeyed for once.

I knelt down to dress each one. I twisted the three dead bolts to the left, making a mental note that they needed some oil. Or maybe the bolts' pesky squeaks would warn me that someone was attempting to break into my apartment. After firmly shutting the door and securing the locks, I followed my small crew down-stairs.

We strode along Dolores Street, stopping at all the fa-miliar trees: Lemon Bottlebrush, Cork Oak, and Strawberry. Flower boxes attached to the fronts of homes held Johnny Jump Ups as well as pink and red Fuchsia. The fog hugged the tops of the buildings. I stopped long enough to zip the front of my coat.

With poop bags in hand, I continued our morning jaunt and, as needed, I dropped the bags in the designated disposal. If reincarnation existed, I wanted to come back as a pampered pup.

I paused at the Steam Heat Coffee Shop's outdoor order window to fill my thermos and pick up the Sunday paper. The dogs' favorite barista, Vinny, appeared. He angled out the window to watch their begging routine. Max plopped on his back and played dead. I lifted Gracey up to the counter so she could get a good sniff of the dog treats someone placed thoughtfully by the window.

Vinny always fell for their act and rewarded them. I turned away from the counter and, through the glass entry, I surveyed the morning crowd. Sunday papers sprawled across tables. Customers sipped coffee, had conversations, and took in the fresh aroma of baked goods.

Then *he* came into view. My heart took an elevator to the basement. Sam appeared by a large window where he stood behind a woman. The sun's rays sliced through the fog and hit him like a spotlight. Though the sunshine added highlights to his auburn hair, his former scruffy look was unchanged. A day-old beard covered his face. Probably took him two hours to put together this casual style. He bent down and struggled with a woman's chair. She was slow to rise as he helped her up. The woman was pregnant.

I couldn't move—I held my breath. Was Sam married and about to become a father? We had discussed having kids, but he said they weren't in his plan. When I told him I was pregnant a year and a half into our relationship, he wasn't excited. I remembered how he held his breath and tightened his chin. He did not accept this news as a happy event. I was one of those women who took birth control pills, but part of the two percent who got pregnant anyway.

He didn't have to worry for long because I miscarried two months later. I should have known the relationship was headed for hell when he took the miscarriage as good news. I staggered through a depression that got in the way of our relationship. His solution for my dark mood was a weekend in Carmel, fine dining, and shopping. Here he was, having coffee at one of our favorite places with a mother-to-be.

The short woman's blonde hair was in a ponytail tucked through the back slit of a baseball cap. A little too casual for Sam's taste. My leg went numb—the shock of seeing them cut off my circulation. I slammed my first into the side of my thigh. This woman could have been me.

He scanned the room and through the window his gaze clashed with mine. When he saw me his grin turned into a dropped jaw. His hand jerked the woman's elbow, and she shot him an angry look. She rested back in the chair. He presented one of his half-smiles, the same he used the night I caught him with a young artist.

I jammed my thermos in my purse along with my newspaper. I was sure as hell not in the mood to be polite. *Screw you, Sam.*

I tugged on the leashes and with dogs in tow, I headed back up the street to my apartment. I was fuming. The dogs kept looking behind them. They must have sensed that something had set me off.

Halfway up the street I heard Sam shout, "Sarah, wait."

I stopped and turned to face him and "Miss Mother." The dogs wrapped their leashes around my ankles. They didn't like the sound of Sam's voice any more than I did. He detested dogs. One time he slapped Gracey away—the mother in me came out—and I swatted his arm.

I almost lost my balance. "What do you want, Sam? I have nothing to say to you." I untangled the leashes holding me hostage. My lips pinched together and my chest tightened.

"Sorry, I didn't mean to upset you. I wanted to introduce you to my sister." He moved closer, nearly dragging the waddling woman.

"Your sister?" I squeezed my eyes shut and shook my head. Three years with this idiot and he never introduced me to her. My hand clenched the leashes.

"Cheryl," he said, "this is Sarah."

My breathing suspended for a split second.

She said, "Nice to meet you. My brother told me how he managed to screw up the best relationship he ever had." She poked him in the ribs—it wasn't playful.

None of us spoke.

What was I supposed to do with that comment? Since I needed to shake off my anger, I drew the leashes closer to my chest. I said, "Yes, he screwed up. I don't mean to be rude because you seem to be a nice person. You also look uncomfortable. It was good meeting you. Goodbye." I tried to turn, but my little captives made it difficult to exit gracefully.

"Would it be okay if I called you some time?" Sam touched my arm.

I flicked his hand away, turned my back to him, and shouted over my shoulder. "Hell no."

He gripped the back of my arm. "Please, I know I screwed up. Seeing you just brought up how much I've missed you." His eyes held a fake expression every time he tried to apologize.

"Let go." I yanked my arm away.

Max snatched the bottom of Sam's slacks and I heard the lovely sound of fabric ripping.

"Sam!" His sister stood with feet apart and hands on hips. "Sarah obviously doesn't want to hear from you. You're an idiot. I'm sorry. He can be a real ass. I think you and I could've been friends, but of course, he kept you hidden. Come on, let's go." She headed in the opposite direction.

Sam backed up a few steps and joined his sister.

Gracey decided to squat and pee.

Good girl.

CHAPTER

The twenty-minute journey back to my apartment included a few swear words under my breath. After we arrived home, all I wanted to do was escape into the Sunday paper and wipe Sam and his sister from the middle of my brain. Despite being together for three years, he never took the time to introduce me to Cheryl.

My hollow mood dissipated. I was finally over him. My fists delivered a celebratory air punch. I unleashed the hounds and plunked down on the couch. My small roommates jumped onto my lap. Max pawed at my sleeve and slid under my arm. Gracey snuggled next to my hips. At least they provided a shelter of safety.

"Thank goodness I have you guys in my life, and Max, good job on Sam's pants." My fingers massaged the tops of their heads.

I resisted sifting through the Sunday paper and snatched the West Coast Swing DVD instead. I flipped the case from front to back and considered tossing it across the room. *Dammit, Liz, you and your "let's do something different" adventures.*

I slid the DVD out of its case, stepped over, and dropped the disc into the player. I picked up the remote and hesitated before I hit play. *Liz, you're trespassing on my Sunday.* Why couldn't she pick something like going to a movie with subtitles? I slumped my shoulders and then surrendered to watching the program.

Two dancers flashed onto the screen. The male appeared in baggy pants, a white shirt with folded-up sleeves, and suspenders. His partner wore a scorching-red, form-fitting dress with a flared hem. They floated into place for the lesson.

Baggy Pants announced, "The West Coast Swing is a high-energy dance. Remember the man's the leader and the woman's the follower."

I planted my feet in front of the TV. The woman was the follower? I had issues with that—Sam led me around for three years.

"Let's practice the basic step called the Sugar Push. It starts with walk, walk, triple step, triple step."

I danced around the front room, repeating "walk, walk, triple step, triple step." I mastered the basics while trying not to trip over the dogs who joined the lesson.

I sat down on the couch and absorbed the rest of the video. Baggy Pants lifted his partner in the air, slid her through his legs, and bounced her onto his left hip.

Might be nice, sliding between Jerard's legs and connecting with his hips.

I triple-stepped and swayed my hips into the kitchen where I toasted a bagel, then spread an extra-thick layer of cream cheese on top. I must have burned some calories in the last hour. I headed over to the bay window and surveyed the street. The neighborhood held that soft Sunday atmosphere.

But my daydreaming switched to live action when I spotted a man in a hoodie. His hands hid in his pockets. A girl strode several feet in front of him. She glanced back at him a couple of times. Every time she turned her head, he would slow his pace.

This did not feel right. I unlatched the lower window, slid it up, and yelled, "Hey!"

The hooded man's head pivoted sharply in my direction, yet I could not see his face. He crossed to the opposite sidewalk and disappeared up 19th Street. The girl climbed onto a bus at the bottom of Dolores Street.

She was safe. A shiver rippled up my spine. My old friend intuition was no longer tucked away in some dark corner of my mind.

12
CHAPTER

The morning drifted into afternoon. Time to give some thought to what to wear tonight. This past week, the last thing on my mind had been to shop for a swing dance outfit. It was going to be all improvisation. I headed toward the bedroom, trailed by two dogs whose nails tapped the hardwood floor.

I separated the accordion closet doors and took inventory of my clothes. Lined up from left to right, the outfits started with white and then went to cream, gray, black, and a few accents of red, burgundy, and blue. When I spotted teal spaghetti straps dangling from a padded hanger, I lifted the dress and dragged it out.

I paused in front of my wall mirror and held the outfit close to my body. *Not too bad, girl.* I imagined my friends whispering, "Where's this little number been hiding?"

After removing it from the hanger and stripping off my sweats, I raised the gown above my head. It slid over my body like extra-virgin olive oil. I ran my hands down my hips, turned sideways, and tapped my stomach. Not as flat as it used to be, but some of my gym work was paying off.

I rotated my back to the mirror and checked out how the low cut "v" made me feel — sexy — something I had not felt in a while.

When I whirled right and left, a teasing flare at the bottom of the dress sent out a signal to the dogs. "Attack!" They jumped off the bed, heading in the direction of this new chew toy. After a slow growl that built into a bark, they organized an assault from front and back.

I bent down and put my hand out, showing them the stop sign. "No — down. I plan to wear this dress tonight and give it the attention it deserves. You're not going to ravage it like it's one of your stuffed animals."

They tucked their tails, retreated, then presented me one of their pathetic looks. I gathered them in a group hug.

After I let go of my team, I took one last glance at the dress. *You nailed it, girl.*

At 3:45 p.m. I finished my Sunday chores, so I had enough time to take a hot bubble bath before I got ready for my date. I decided to wear my Irish red hair down. Most of the time my hair reminded me of an old cartoon.

The character would stick his finger in an electrical out-
let and his hair would stand up on end. Tonight,
thankfully, it relaxed into soft curls. I added a 1940s
touch by tying a sheer silver scarf under my hair and
accenting it with a bow.

I dug through my aunt's jewelry box and found a
pair of pearl earrings, a must in the Forties. I dabbed
rosewater behind each ear, adding a few drops between
my breasts and finishing my ensemble with low-heeled,
open-toed silver shoes. I'd considered wearing flats, but
because Jerard was slightly taller, I wanted to take ad-
vantage of the rare opportunity to add a few inches to
my height. The dogs lined up—I was ready for inspection.

"What do you think?" I asked.

Their heads leaned left.

"No comment, huh?"

They waddled away. No snacks? No interest.

I took one more glance in the mirror and applied a deep
red lipstick. At half-past five the apartment speaker
buzzed. *Jerard, you're right on time.* I held down the respond button. "Hello."

"Hi, Sarah." His voice expressed a deep, velvet quality.

I braced my back against the wall and let out a long,
slow breath. "I'll be right down." The dogs waited at the
door for our guest. "Sorry, guys. I'm not ready for Jerard
to meet you unruly children."

I treated them to one last cookie and stepped into the hall. The murdered girls on the news had me feeling a little jumpy. I made sure to double-check each dead bolt before heading down the stairs.

I opened the lobby door and paused to make a deep study of Jerard. He wore pleated, cream-colored pants; a white shirt with a buttoned-down collar; and a set of wild-colored suspenders—a swing dancer all the way. His highly polished Italian loafers clashed a bit with his ensemble. He observed me for a moment without saying a word. My face heated up a few degrees.

He tipped his head. "That dress flatters every part of you." He glanced down; his gaze landed on my small cleavage.

I hoped my new push-up bra was holding to its promise. My self-confidence was returning like a long-lost friend. "It's been a while since I've dressed up."

Mrs. Ackermann, my eighty-year-old neighbor, came up the steps as we started down. Mr. and Mrs. Ackermann watched Max and Gracey during the day, and she took them out for a couple of outings. I insisted on paying them for dog sitting to help supplement their income.

"It's so nice seeing you going out again, Sarah. Now be careful, you two. You've heard about the awful killings of those poor girls. You're not the killer are you, young man? Because you could sure kill me with those green eyes of yours." She snickered.

Jerard did not respond; instead, his focus switched away up the street.

I bent forward. "Okay, enough flirting. What would your husband say?"

"He told me I could always peek but never touch. I'll use the set of keys you gave me and take the pups out for a short visit through the neighborhood before we go to bed."

"They always look forward to the walks, but I think it's more about the peanut butter cookies you give them when you get back."

"Good night. Have fun." She headed up the steps.

Jerard offered me his arm. "Ready for an evening of swing?"

I tucked my arm under his. "As ready as I'll ever be." Part of me wanted to run back upstairs to the safety of my apartment and two familiar faces. Mrs. Ackermann continued to stare at us. Her eyes squinted.

The town car was parked in front of my building. Joe, the chauffeur, appeared again at the back door. His eyes toured me from head to toe; his hand hesitated for a moment on the handle.

I would have to remember to wear this dress more often. I wondered if he had someone in his life. He always looked so distant, maybe sad.

He swung the door wide. The cuffs of his white dress shirt were frayed, unlike Jerard's clothes that appeared to be cleaned by a professional. Jerard cleared his throat abruptly, and we slid across the back seat. Joe merged the town car into traffic; Jerard's hand rested on my knee—his touch brought on a surge of excitement.

In what direction was this night headed? Would I

allow myself to follow? I would definitely welcome a goodnight kiss.

My eyes met Joe's in the rearview mirror. His gaze lingered more than a few seconds. *Are you flirting with me, Joe?*

A few minutes before 6:00 p.m., the town car slowed into the twenty-minute loading zone in front of the Just Dance Studio in the Mission District off 24th Street. Joe put the car in neutral. I focused on the studio doors draped with red velvet curtains.

Jerard offered his hand to me as I exited the back seat. He glanced back at Joe who remained by the car. "You can go now. I'll call you when we're finished."

"Yes, sir." Joe hesitated before he turned to leave, and I swear he covered a smile with his hand.

Jerard observed Joe until he was back in the driver's seat. His forehead crease deepened; his eyes scanned the car as it moved back into traffic. He opened the studio door, and I took in the steep, narrow stairs leading upward. Thousands of shoes had worn down the wood. Arriving at the top, I brushed my hand across the red velvet curtain. Café tables lined the perimeter of the dance floor.

White linen cloths draped each table. Centerpieces featured a crystal vase holding a single red rose amid sprays of baby's breath. Recorded swing music played in the background. My adrenaline shot up a few degrees. This music was kidnapping my hips, convincing them to move from right to left. Music always brought energy to my veins.

My friends assembled around a table at the far side of the room. I raised a hand and caught Liz's attention. She rose and signaled. A red dress draped her figure. The rest of our group examined the creative Forties outfits they'd put together. Were they auditioning for community theater?

A hand swept my back. There was a jolt again. Jerard steered me toward my friends.

The group said their hellos, and during this moment I sensed all eyes on me. They checked me out from floor to ceiling while I shifted from one foot to another. Was my bra showing? Did I have my dress on backward?

Liz broke the silence. "Okay, guys. I know we haven't seen Sarah this dressed up in a long time, but would you mind moving your slack jaws into a closed position?"

"Sarah, oh hell, you look hot." Bill's face reddened like an overripe tomato.

Nicole rested her head on Bill's shoulder. "Take a few deep breaths. Remember me? Your wife?"

"We should dress up more often," I said. Thank goodness the lights started to dim, and the music was getting louder.

13

CHAPTER

A pool of light spilled onto the dance floor. The music's rapid beats stirred my body. The two teachers from the DVD danced into the center of the room with speed and precision. They turned and, after lifting her, the man threw his partner between his legs; she slid through and popped up onto both feet. She performed on two-inch heels. They took a bow and we applauded. I hoped they didn't expect us to accomplish those steps by the end of the evening.

The teachers, Michelle and Greg, joined our group. Michelle took Jerard's arm and Greg led Nicole to the center of the highly polished wooden floor. The rest of us followed like a herd of frightened calves.

"Welcome to a night of West Coast Swing," Greg said. "We'll review the basic Sugar Push step. Hopefully, everyone studied their DVDs."

We split into two groups. The women lined up behind Michelle, and she demonstrated the basic steps. After a half hour the couples formed a large circle facing their partners; Michelle and Greg remained in the center.

"Remember men, you are the leaders, and you ladies are the followers." Greg's height seemed to increase an inch as he said this.

Okay, Greg, you're in charge. Calm down.

Michelle rolled her eyes. Did she have problems being the follower?

"Everyone!" Greg quieted the noisy group. "The men offer the women a palms-up left hand, and the girls place what I like to call the 'knuckle punch,' right hand into the palm." Greg formed a tight fist.

Knuckle punch—I liked that term. Gave me a bit of an edge, not completely letting the man lead.

Greg extended his hand to Michelle. He drew her in so closely only a wafer-thin space remained between them.

I stepped toward Jerard and he lured me into his familiar heat.

"We're going to practice the Sugar Push. Step, step, triple step, triple step. I'll count aloud, and after we've mastered that, we'll add music." Greg moved through the dance floor, demonstrating the steps.

Jerard led me around the room, step, step, triple step, triple step.

I wanted to collapse into his arms, but my feet seemed wrapped in seaweed. I eyeballed them. *Come on, you two can do better than that.*

Greg's voice broke my concentration. "Keep your eyes

on your partner, not your feet."

The overhead lighting cast a candlelit effect on those emerald eyes. His lips were so close my breasts fused with his chest. If he brought me in for a long deep kiss, I would not object.

Jerard whispered. "I used to watch my feet. If I tried hard enough, I believed I could convince them to do the right thing."

I said, "Maybe you could converse with mine." *Or you could whisk me away to the coatroom and we could have some crazy sex. No one would miss us. What do you think?*

Greg counted as the circle repeated the Sugar Push. He clapped his annoying hands. "Ok, everyone, your attention please."

Partners disconnected and the entire group relaxed, congratulating each other on their success in mastering the basic step.

Michelle stepped in front of Greg. "We're now going to practice with music by Glenn Miller." He seemed a bit miffed at her taking over.

Go on, Michelle, give him a good knuckle punch.

"Return to your beginning position." Greg jerked Michelle around to face him.

He reminded me so much of Sam who constantly dragged and coerced me to dance under his direction.

Jerard and I stepped in and faced each other. After he offered his open palm, my breathing slowed, and my body followed.

The music started. Jerard lulled me into a comfortable rhythm.

For the first time in so long, I trusted my body to move where it wanted to go. My maneuvers were lighter, not restricted, as if I pried open a stuck window and let the cool air enter.

"Time to change partners," Greg announced. Was he taking over again?

I didn't want to leave Jerard. As we moved to our next partner, Jerard delayed our departure by sliding his hand down my arm. Then he was off to another woman. Ten other couples participated, including our group, so it was going to be a while before Jerard and I were joined again.

My next partner wore a canary yellow Zoot suit with a jacket that fell to his knees and shoulder pads that bulged like small mattresses. His shirt opened to the third button, and his gold chains and hairy chest assaulted my vision. His shoulders rounded like a tiger ready to pounce. Jeez, how much cologne did he put on?

Thank goodness Paul was my third partner. He took me in his arms and jumped right into more questions. "I have to ask." He cleared his throat. "What do you think of Jerard? There's something about him. The guy might be hiding who he really is."

"What is it with the two of you?" My words spilled out before I could catch them.

"I don't want to see you hurt. I know how long it took for you to get over Sam. Maybe I'm being overprotective.

I'll work on it." He shrugged his shoulders.

I nodded. "I appreciate your support, but I'm moving forward in my life and I have to start trusting again." But I wasn't convinced he would let go so effortlessly.

Thirty minutes elapsed before I returned to Jerard. "I feel like we survived some kind of natural disaster," I said. His hand grazed my cheek.

Greg's voice interrupted our moment. "Very nice. Let's take a break. We've provided a nice red wine and ice water on each table."

Jerard's hand drifted away and we turned back to listen to Greg's voice.

He said, "We're going to add the Sugar Tuck next."

Crap, I just mastered the first step. Panic slithered back in. I gnawed the inside of my cheek.

We returned to our table where our group sat down for a much-needed rest. A pitcher of water and a carafe of red wine glistened. Paul filled our glasses.

I put my hand over my glass. "I'll stick to water." I did not need my size tens colliding with each other on the dance floor.

Liz and Nicole sat side by side, their shoulders connected. They shared something amusing. A moment of melancholy swept over me — I missed sitting next to them.

"Are you two comparing notes about our dance techniques?" Paul put an arm around Liz and drew her close.

"No, honey. We're just trying to figure out how to skip Mr. Gold Chains next time around."

I paused, thinking. They were such an important part of my life.

Nicole rubbed her neck. "He shoved and dragged me around so hard, I thought I was going to be hurled out into the lobby if he let go. I may have to see the chiropractor tomorrow."

"Let me tell you," I said, "with his five-foot-three-inch height, he was level with Lucy and Ethel here." I pointed to my breasts. "When I saw him coming in for a landing, I locked both elbows and held him back."

Jerard put his head in both hands, obviously amused.

"Does that mean your guys rate a ten?" Bill asked.

"In comparison to Mr. Gold Chains, yes," I said.

Nicole hooted.

"Sarah, are you enjoying the Swing?" Jerard's amusement settled. He rested his elbow on the table, his chin cradled in his palm.

I considered grabbing his hand, tracking down a dark secluded corner, and . . . . *Wow, I believe the old Sarah's been resuscitated.* "I am. I guess I should give credit to Liz." I reached across and placed my hand over hers. "I wasn't excited about your plan for this month, but thanks. This has definitely been an entertaining diversion."

She winked at me, "How about scuba diving next month?"

There was a moment, just before we hit the brick wall, when everyone figured out she was kidding. Not me. I could see us lining up for our rental equipment.

Jerard scooted his chair closer, lured me in, and ignited the match. My face was close to his hair with the light lemon scent. Instead of resisting, I coasted into him. It was comfortable; I wondered about the taste of his kiss.

Paul rocked back in his chair. "Jerard, tell us a little more about yourself."

Dammit, Paul. Jerard's lips were just about to caress mine and you had to call "cut" to the scene I was plotting.

"What would you like to know?" As Jerard took a sip of water, the ice cubes hit the side of his glass. His voice sounded flat.

"Where'd you live before San Francisco?"

Liz spoke up. "He already told you that last night at dinner. Weren't you listening?"

"You said you lived in Los Angeles and before that New York. Right?" Paul leaned back, angling the chair on its back legs.

"That's correct." Jerard offered no more.

Was Paul trying to trip him? My knees bounced under the table. I kind of hoped Paul would lose his balance and go flying backwards. When was he going to stop this line of questioning? Paul tipped his chair forward and the two men engaged. Their shoulders rose a bit higher. I fidgeted with my right earring. Was this where the duel at dawn came in?

"Where'd you live before New York?" Paul asked.

"Stop it!" Liz shoved her hand against Paul's shoulder

with such force, our group seemed to lift and land in their seats. "This is not an interrogation room, it's a dance class." She thrust her chair back so hard that Paul had to shoot out a hand to prevent her falling.

The room suspended for a moment, and then a voice brought it back to life. "Dancers," Michelle shouted, breaking up the male Sugar Push that was going on at our table. "Please, return to the floor."

We headed back to dance. What a relief—no more questions.

Paul and Liz stepped in front of us. Paul shifted his attention over his shoulder; his fierce eyes aimed at Jerard. He appeared to meet Paul's stare. A grin formed at the edge of his lips. Then Paul disengaged and refocused on me. His lips separated for a moment, then closed.

What is it, Paul? My deep-rooted trust issues crept back in like unwelcome intruders.

14
CHAPTER

A few minutes later we assumed our places in a circle around Michelle and Greg. Waiters cleared the tables of empty glasses. Paul and Jerard's banter softened as Michelle dimmed the lights.

"This step is called the Front Sugar Tuck," Greg announced. "You continue the basic step, but we'll add a turn for the women."

Sparks traveled up my arms as Jerard moved his hand across the bare skin of my upper back. We performed the basic step, and he guided me into the turn. He attempted to rotate my body, but my hips locked up.

"You need to relax," he said.

"I am relaxed!" I snapped.

"Let's try again." His voice was gentle. "Try and let me lead you into the turn. Trust me."

Trust you? It wasn't going to be that easy. I took a deep

breath. As I exhaled, Jerard spun me into a smooth rotation. My body finally unlocked. Cool ocean air filled my lungs.

"Perfect!" Jerard shot me a grin. "You did it!"

"Let's do that again," I said. While we danced for the next half hour, my entire being felt freed from a prison cell. We no longer battled through the instructions. Instead, we traveled through the room with no doubts, no second guessing who was in charge, moving through space as one. A rhythm developed between the two of us, and I welcomed it.

Michelle and Greg danced inside the circle. Their motions were effortless, light, as if their feet did not touch the floor.

I took a risk and loosened my hips. We developed a pulse as if swimming through warm water.

That was when it happened: Cinderella's elegant coach turned back into a pumpkin.

Jerard's Italian leather loafers stumbled—his heel landed on my right big toe. "Ow!" A piercing pain. My eyes watered. *Well, I guess my hopes of becoming a professional swing dancer have just plummeted.*

I tried to step outside the circle, but it was too late, causing the group to come to a domino halt.

Jerard wrapped an arm around my waist and helped me back to our table. I sat down and he kneeled in front of me, embracing both my hands. "I guess you'll be auditioning a new dance partner." He squeezed his eyes shut.

"It isn't that bad." I said. But when I eased off my right shoe, the throbbing increased.

Michelle appeared with an ice bag.

"Thank you, Michelle. I'll be fine." I took the bag. "Go back. I'll enjoy watching you and Greg." She returned to class, her hips swaying side to side. She certainly knew how to get men's attention.

Jerard placed his chair in front of mine. He withdrew the ice bag from my hand and placed it on my toe. "I have to tell you, Sarah, you're a wonderful partner. Let's try another class sometime." He rested my leg on his lap and massaged the back of my calf. My toe hurt, not my calf. *Oh, shut up, Sarah.* His gentle hand on my leg felt pretty damn good.

Although my toe swelled, I didn't want him to stop. My friends gathered around. After I assured them I was okay, I told them to return to the dance floor. We watched the group for about a half an hour. Jerard pointed out that Mr. Gold Chains was on the prowl.

My mind debated. We were doing so well, and then this had to happen. Why was I beating myself up? After all, he was the one who stepped on my toe. I wanted to go home, take some aspirin, and climb into bed. I put my hand on his shoulder. "I'm sorry to ruin our evening, but would you mind taking me to my place?"

"I'll call Joe to bring the car around." He punched in the number on his cell, circled his arm around my waist, and helped me up from the chair.

We headed toward the entrance, and I tightened my grip on Jerard's arm. I tried not to put too much pressure on my foot, so I had to hop a bit. Michelle and Greg paused the music, thanked us for coming, and said they hoped we would come back for another lesson at no cost. My friends left the circle; they came over to persuade us to stay.

"I think it's best I go home and soak my toe. Go back and enjoy the rest of the evening." My voice wavered.

"We'll call you when we get home to make sure you're okay." Nicole said.

The music started up again, and I watched as the group tackled the Sugar Tuck.

I glanced at Jerard. Would there be a third date? We were at the door when I heard Paul's voice behind me.

"Hey, Jerard, I'm working on a case that deals with the art world. You mind if I pick your brain? Could you come down to the precinct one day this week?"

"Let me check my calendar and I'll call you." Jerard's arm tensed around my waist.

"Here's my card. If I'm not in, just leave a message and I'll call back." Paul appeared about to say something else when Liz's hand snatched his arm. "If you don't want divorce papers served to you right here and now, you'll return to the dance floor." Liz did not seem to be kidding.

We headed down the stairs. "You going to take Paul up on his invitation?" I asked.

"I might. Could be interesting." He nudged me.

It might be entertaining for him, but I found it a bit unnerving. Why wouldn't Paul ease up on Jerard?

It took a few minutes to hobble down the stairs where Joe waited by the car. When we entered the back seat, I did my best to squirm across without looking like a seal mounting a wooden plank at Fishermen's Wharf. Jerard slid in next to me and extended his arm around my shoulder. One minute I was on the plank, and the next my head settled into the soft curve of his neck.

He raised my chin. "Now that I have officially retired as your dance partner, I think a nice dinner out might be the way to go next time. I thought I was an experienced dancer. Guess I was nervous."

I drew back and flashed him a smile. What did he have to be nervous about? I was the one with monkeys doing headstands in my stomach. No, this guy wasn't the nervous type.

"My toe will survive." I rested my head against the leather seat. I needed to slow down a bit. "Dinner would be nice."

The trip back to my apartment went by so fast that when the car stopped, it startled me.

Joe emerged outside my window. A blast of cold air permeated the car, reminding me I should have brought a coat. Jerard helped me out, but when I slid across the seat, my dress drifted up my leg. I took Jerard's hand and static passed between us.

He beamed. "We've sparked some electricity."

My heartbeat ran a marathon.

Joe leaned in and offered his right elbow for extra support. How thoughtful. I accepted his arm for support and did my best to stand. Jerard swatted him away like a fly, so Joe lowered his hand.

"Sorry, Joe," Jerard said. "I have her now."

His apology, stiff and cold, did not sound sincere. There had been tension between Paul and Jerard, and now I sensed the same with Joe and Jerard. Did he have a quick temper? Was I reading too much into this?

"Good night." I touched his shoulder.

"Good night, Ma'am. Take care." His fading smile lacked its earlier energy and he disappeared into the car.

I handed Jerard my keys, and we trekked through the lobby and up the stairs. I could hear the dogs' opera. *Should I invite him in?*

His forehead crinkled. "Sounds like there are some dogs happy to hear footsteps."

"My two dachshunds are at it again."

"Two?" He rubbed his head and his eyes widened.

I would wait and introduce them another time. I just wanted to soak my toe, take some Motrin, and hit the sack.

CHAPTER

Outside my door I pointed to the purple, yellow, and red keys that unlocked the three dead bolts. "My aunt insisted on having these installed when we moved in."

"Sounds like she was cautious." Jerard unlocked all three while continuing to support my waist.

I swiveled to face him. "I think I'll say goodnight and soak my toe in some ice water. I had a wonderful time, but I'm really tired."

"Hmm, you sound as if we're not going to see each other after tonight." His hands cradled my face. "Let's try this again. How about a nice dinner on the wharf some night? No dancing, just sitting and getting to know more about each other."

My self-confidence restored, I placed my hands on his cheeks. "I like that idea. Let's go some place casual."

"Perfect. I'll call you in the morning to see how you are."

His arms encircled me tightly, and he drew me into a kiss that turned my body into liquid. The kiss started slow and soft, and then plunged deeper as he parted my lips with his tongue. Maybe I should invite him in. Then I heard scratching and growls at the bottom of my door.

"Good night, Sarah." I loved how he said my name, throaty and sexy.

"Good night." I sounded a little like Lauren Bacall from the movie *To Have and Have Not*. Should I have asked him if he knew how to whistle?

I watched him continue down the stairs. My inner voice yelled, "Don't go."

He stopped and swung his head around. "Go inside. I need to hear all three dead bolts. Everyone's pretty concerned about the serial killer. You need to be careful."

Why would he bring that up now? I rubbed my hands up and down my arms, trying to rid myself of chills. "Good night, Jerard." I went inside, twisted the locks, and heard the reassuring click, click, click.

Our bodies sculpted together. I felt his heat against my body—he was ready. Jerard slid his hands around my waist and up to caress my breasts. I turned over and kissed him good morning. He slid on top of me and . . . the piercing sound of the alarm demolished the moment.

Well, that was quite a dream. My time with Jerard last night affected me. My sleep mates tickled my neck with their wet noses, bringing me back to reality.

"Hey, you guys." I fluffed my pillow and tucked the blanket under my arms. Two wet noses crawled up from under the blankets and rested under my arm. My concentration returned to Jerard. *No matter how old we are, we never stop wondering if the guy will call or make us wait.*

I checked the alarm clock. Monday morning, time to get ready for work. I would love to call in sick. The Van Ness movie theater was playing Jimmy Stewart movies all day. A day of buttered popcorn and Jimmy would be, as my aunt used to say, groovy. My boss would never believe me if I told him I was suffering from extreme lust. I resigned myself to getting up.

I placed my suffering foot down on the cold wood. Although the swelling had gone down, my toe turned a lovely shade of purple. I headed to the kitchen for our morning ritual: coffee, feed the dogs, a quick run with them down to the backyard, and a shower. While in the shower I missed three phone calls—Nicole and Liz—and to my surprise—Jerard. I skipped the first two and listened to his recording.

"Is your toe better this morning? I hope you don't mind, but last night Nicole cornered me and said you were going to have a singing debut Saturday night at Courtney's. She said you've been studying with a singing coach for three years. I kind of invited myself. You're full of surprises. See you Saturday. Or should I say, break a leg? Isn't that what showbiz people say? Bye." One click ended the message.

Gracey and Max were at my feet. I thought for a moment. He was a bit forward, inviting himself to my performance. I wasn't excited about Nicole including him without asking me first. I was nervous enough about singing in front of an audience. Now I had Jerard in the mix. Wait a minute, why was I being so edgy? *Knock it off. Your voice is strong. Okay – it's settled.*

I survived the typical Monday at work. I took the rest of the week off by using vacation time. Tom called from Courtney's to ask if we could get together on Wednesday to go over a possible singing contract. He said he had a huge surprise for me. We agreed to meet at Stow Lake in Golden Gate Park at 9:00 a.m. The dogs needed a change of scenery. They loved lifting a leg on a tree, sniffing other dogs' butts, and chasing squirrels.

The traffic on Wednesday was bad as usual. I knew I had hit commute time, so I decided to leave at 8:00 a.m. to head for the park. I dressed the dogs in their winter sweaters and attached their leashes. I threw a down jacket over my Warriors sweatshirt and well-worn sweatpants. I led the pups to my ancient Volkswagen parked as usual at a nearby curb.

The dogs entered their back-seat kennel obediently, and I started the car. I took Pine Street over to Masonic Avenue and made my way to Martin Luther King Drive. It was early, so I found plenty of parking when I arrived at the lake. I unloaded my tail-wagging friends from the car.

Although we favored Stow Lake as one of our weekend hangouts, I decided to take the dogs out in the middle of the week, rather than stick to our same old schedule. Besides, I was excited about Tom's contract offer. I couldn't wait to sing again. The Boat House came into view. I had wonderful memories of renting paddleboats and snacking on cotton candy with my aunt and uncle, and my dentist's full-blown lectures following those adventures.

16
CHAPTER

I enjoyed our slow pace, inhaling the fragrance of euca-
lyptus, Monterey pine, and cypress. Early morning
joggers ran by. A few tourists wore backpacks, ready for
their trek through Golden Gate Park.

I spotted Tom waving his arm. The dogs tugged me
toward him. "Good morning." I took hold of his arm
and looked into his soft blue eyes while my right hand
held the twitching leashes.

"Hey, beautiful." He kissed my cheek. Tom's dress
code did not match the rest of us in the park. He wore a
white, starched, long-sleeved shirt, sport coat, wool
scarf, khaki pants, and shoes that would need polishing
after a tromp through the grass.

The dogs sniffed his legs, jumped up, and got dirt all
over his light-colored slacks. He poked the dogs away
with his foot — how annoying.

"Dammit!" He tried to brush off the dirt, but it clung to his pants.

"Sorry, but you need to invest in a pair of sweats if you're going to meet me in the park."

He wore so much product in his blond hair the wind had no chance of relocating even one strand. Was he more comfortable in his restaurant than outdoors?

Tom said, "I don't do sweats. Besides, November's not the greatest time for a visit to the park. I hope the fog lifts a little. I should've worn my overcoat."

"Enough chit chat. Tell me about this surprise." We headed along the lake and I heard the familiar splash of the waterfall near the boathouse.

"I invited Lorraine Stark, owner of The Only Jazz Club on Third Street, to sit in on your performance."

"You did?" Fear crawled up my legs like overgrown branches.

"She listened to one of your tapes and she's interested. I wasn't sure I wanted to share your talent, but I think this would be a good career move for you. I don't want to hold you back. Remember, I'm the one who persuaded you to sing at my restaurant." He nudged my side.

"You think I'm ready?"

"Stop second-guessing. Jump in and sing. Your voice coach said you were ready years ago. You know Mrs. Campbell wouldn't lie to you."

I was not paying attention to the dogs, so when I relaxed my hold, Max jerked away. His leash slipped through my fingers, and he raced toward a stand of trees. "Max! Stop! Come back here now." I handed Tom the other leash. He held it a good distance away from his body while I sprinted after the escapee.

But my attention was quickly diverted: a group of police had strung yellow tape around a small area. Inside the perimeter a green tarp covered something against the trunk of a cypress. The edge of the tarp was in between Max's teeth, and he yanked hard.

A few moments earlier I heard birds chirping, children crying, and joggers pounding the pavement. Then all sound vanished. My vision shrank to the size of a narrow tunnel: she was propped against a conifer as if absorbing the view of the lake. Her head lolled to one side, and her skin was pale as chalk. Deep red lipstick smeared across her full, cherub-shaped lips. A red scarf was tied around her neck, and the breeze lifted its ends. Her dead eyes bulged, and I had the sensation of falling right into them. A box with a red bow rested on her lap—it appeared to be a box of chocolates, but I couldn't be sure.

I tried to nab Max, but he was next to her body, sniffing. "Max, no. Come!" The echo of my own voice smacked me hard. A policeman collected Max's leash and handed it to me. "Ma'am, you need to leave this area. You've already contaminated the crime scene."

I tried to move. Were my feet encased in cement? I stood before this woman—her life was over. How would you tell parents their child had been murdered? I remembered the news about the serial killer moving up the coast. All indications suggested he headed toward the Bay Area.

Was the killer here watching? I scanned the park. Would one of us be next?

Tom stood outside the yellow tape near a policewoman. Gracey tugged at the end of the leash and he tried to control her. "What's going on?" He shouted to me over the heads of the gathering crowd.

I slammed through the onlookers and seized his hand. "A woman's dead." I could hardly breathe. My legs did not support me well and I might have thrown up. Tom's arms held me while Max and Gracey whined faintly and moved closer to my ankles.

"Jeez. Come on, let's get out of here." Tom escorted me and my dog crew back to our car.

I placed my hand on the hood for support. "That poor woman. It's almost as if she'd been staged there, the way she was propped up. So pasty and that garish lipstick—I can't get her face out of my mind." My insides twisted. Could I make it home without getting sick?

"Want me to follow you to your apartment?" Tom asked.

"No. I need to go home and sort out these images." I shoved my hand into my pocket and retrieved my car key. My hand shook as I twisted the key in the door lock. I loaded the dogs in their kennel, then held onto the car door for a moment. Tears raced down my cheeks.

Tom grasped my shoulders. "I've never seen you this shook up before. Are you sure you're okay to drive?"

I raised my chin. "Do you think this might be the work of the serial killer the news is reporting?"

He looked in the direction of the dead woman. "Who knows? Could be."

"That means that women in this city are at risk, including me." A jogger passed by too closely — I flinched.

"If that's the case, you better be damn careful. I don't want to have to find a replacement singer for your debut."

"You think this is funny? A girl is murdered and you're making a joke? God, Tom." I reached for the door handle.

"No, no, I'm sorry. You know how words fall out of my mouth sometimes without me thinking. I didn't mean to make light of this. It's horrible and I can see how it scared you. Listen, we can get together another time and discuss the contract. I think you need to get some rest. Do you think you'll be okay for the performance Saturday?"

I knew he was saying something, but I caught only a few of his words. My mind floated in and out before the face of death.

"I'll be fine. I need to leave." I got into the car and started the engine. I couldn't seem to shift into first gear; I sat there staring out the window. How odd — a woman was murdered, yet the rest of the world continued on with their plans.

CHAPTER 17

I took off the dogs' jackets and fed both a treat before settling on the sofa in front of the bay window. The neighborhood was oblivious to what I had seen. The dead girl's face materialized before me. Beads of sweat formed on my upper lip; my breathing grew erratic—signs of a full-blown panic attack. I got to my feet and paced. If only I could remember everything my therapist taught me.

I hummed and let the vibration in my vocal cords soothe my anxious nerves. I took slow deep breaths, but that didn't help. Thoughts of the murder scene emerged like a tidal wave. Did someone she love kill her? Did she trust, only to be lied to and murdered? Could this happen to me? Could I trust, only to have it stolen once again?

My mind drifted into a new lane. What did I know about Jerard? He just moved here; what if he was the killer? His behavior seemed normal. But what made a killer stand out from the crowd? I swallowed hard, causing a scratching sound in my throat.

When I sat on the couch, the dogs jumped up and settled around my hips. I'd seen a woman's corpse, something out of a nightmare. I picked up Max and held him close until he burrowed his head into my neck. I drifted farther into the cushions. Maybe I could make my body as small as possible, just disappear. I closed my eyes. If only I could erase the vision of the dead girl's pallid skin and smeared lipstick.

I fetched the phone off the coffee table and punched in Nicole's number. No answer. I tried Liz's home phone, but again, no one picked up. That was it. I'd share with them after I performed Saturday night. I had to keep a clear head. While rubbing my neck, I shuffled through a fashion magazine, stopping at an ad for brightly colored foulards. The scarf—the red scarf. I let the magazine fall to my lap. How had I forgotten about the wrap tied around the dead woman's neck?

I sat up and the magazine slid to the floor. "The scarf! Did he strangle her with it?" My hands shook.

Max placed his paws in my lap and glanced up.

"It's okay, buddy. I'm just thinking out loud." I picked up Max again and held him tight. "Thanks for watching over me."

I put him down and decided to sing, the one thing that would calm my nerves. I had a performance Saturday and that was what I needed to concentrate on right now. *Don't give up on the dream.* I set up the microphone, inserted the CD with the arrangement I'd pre-recorded, hit play, and blasted the fear out of my lungs.

After a fitful night's sleep I cracked open the front door and retrieved the rolled-up newspaper on the mat. I started to read it, but after rejecting the idea of seeing the murdered woman's photo on the front page, I tossed it on the kitchen counter. Instead, I stepped toward the coffee pot, then paused midway. Maybe I should see if there was any news about the murder. Maybe they arrested the killer.

As I suspected, her murder made the front page. Thursday's banner headline read, "Young Woman Found Dead in Golden Gate Park," above a photo of the taped-off crime scene. Thank God they didn't show a photo of her tormented face. Her pale skin and empty eyes remained fixed in my mind.

The accompanying article implied the murder might be linked to the serial killer the police sought. I read more details about the suspect's profile. His pattern was to travel up the coast and the police tied him to a murder in Los Angeles. Jerard was from L.A.

I dropped the paper. What did I know about him? Not much. Horrible thoughts hurtled through my mind. "Stop it, Sarah." I said aloud.

I heard the clicking of paws running toward me in the kitchen "Sorry, guys. It's just me going a bit crazy again." I filled their food bowls, then continued reading the story, tormenting myself. The dead woman hadn't yet been identified. No purse or other personal effects were found at the scene, and a search was underway for the names of recently missing young women. I set down the paper and grabbed the edge of the counter.

Maybe I should have a nightly check-in with my friends to make sure we all arrived home safely and remembered to lock every window and door. I put my hand on my throat and the image of that red scarf popped up again. Something touched my ankle and I jumped hard, sending Max racing for the front room. I hurried after him. "I'm sorry, Max." I whispered, cuddling him while he nuzzled his head under my chin.

Still holding Max, I crumpled the paper. *Enough!* I placed the dog on the floor and headed back to the kitchen where I pounded my fists on the counter. I had to put all my energy into Saturday's performance. I tossed the newspaper in the trash. I may have let Sam screw with my mind, but I would not let the murder distract me from what I wanted to do. I stomped over to the CD player. My thumping feet started my motor. I loaded the rehearsal disc and began a vocal warm up. No one would take this away from me.

Saturday morning arrived. I went to yoga to calm my nerves. Every time my eyes closed, the face of the murdered woman reappeared. I did not want to talk to anyone about what I had seen for fear it would come to life again. *Get this performance over with and then tell them.* My focus needed to be one hundred percent on tonight's performance. I might as well look good when they find me passed out from stage fright.

So I booked a massage, manicure, and pedicure. Then I spent the remainder of the afternoon rehearsing my song list. I assumed Jerard would attend the performance, but I wasn't sure. I hadn't received another phone call from him, only one message when he'd invited himself.

I did my best not to sit by the phone and pine like a teenager. I should have called him. *Get over the rejection and cut my losses. Okay, brain, SHUT UP.* I used one of my relaxation methods. I breathed in, held my breath for a few seconds, and exhaled. That didn't help. I did a few stretches. Nada. Zip.

At 6:00 p.m. I headed across the hall to drop off the dogs at the Ackermanns'. When the dogs started barking, Mrs. Ackermann greeted me at the door. She bent to give Max and Gracey a treat.

"Break a leg tonight as they say in show biz." Mr. Ackermann stood tall behind his wife, his face beaming. "Promise to tell us about your big night." His gray beard rubbed my face as he pecked my cheek. I invited them to the performance, but over the years the arthritis in his knees worsened. He was pretty much housebound.

I said, "Of course. I'm not sure when I'll get home." Thank goodness they were here to help with my pups.

Mrs. Ackermann placed her hand on my shoulder. "Let the pooches spend the night—go have yourself a good time."

"What would I do without you two?" I hugged them and leaned down to give the dogs one last tussle.

I sauntered downstairs in my two-inch silver heels and a three-quarter length peacock-blue dress, showing all the curves I cultivated, thanks to my battles at the gym. I treated myself by calling a town car service to pick me up. That night I wasn't sliding into the back of a cab, taking a chance of sitting on someone's leftover cream-filled donut. I took in the view of the city as I headed to Courtney's. The bright lights excited me. Soon I'd be at the mic, finally releasing the voice I'd hidden for too many years.

18
CHAPTER

At 6:30 p.m. sharp I arrived at the restaurant. Tom, arms wide, greeted me at the entrance. "Okay, you need to wear that dress every day for the rest of your life." He stepped back. "Wow, Sarah. Are you sure we shouldn't give dating another try?"

"Okay, Mr. Smooth, if you can manage to get me on that stage, I'll pay for a date that includes a hundred-dollar bottle of wine." He held the door and I glanced around the room. All the chairs and tables near the stage were filled. People, many deep in conversation, were having drinks. A few checked me out. I heard laughter from the restaurant behind the Golden Gate doors. A thin layer of moisture popped out on the palms of my hands.

I spotted my friends and Jerard seated in the middle of the room. He had come. They did a thumbs up and I tossed one back. I would not go over to their table. I was nervous enough, so I would visit with them after the performance. After I stepped over to the bar, I scooped up a paper napkin and wiped my hands dry.

It was 7:00 p.m. Show time. The lights dimmed. Tom mounted the stage and prepared the mic. Audience chatter fell to a few whispers. "Good evening," he said. "I would like to introduce to you—Sarah Soon, a dear friend and fantastic singer. She has privileged Courtney's with her debut performance. Enjoy."

The crowd noise softened to a murmur. I set down the mineral water I'd been sipping and then moved in slow motion toward the stage. My big moment was happening.

Mrs. Campbell, my pianist, gently squeezed my arm. I stepped onto the stage and wrapped my hands around the cold metal of the mic. Mrs. Campbell hit the first few notes. As my lips parted the entire room went dark. Had the power gone out? What was going on? I couldn't move. My body hardened into a solid piece of marble.

Tom stepped up behind me and whispered. "Don't worry, this happens on occasion." He spoke to the audience. "Listen everyone, I have to go and kick the shit out of the power breaker box. It'll only take a minute. The next round is on the house." The crowd cheered. He disappeared through the double doors.

Mrs. Campbell came up beside me. "Relax your shoulders." Her voice soothed me.

The noise level of the audience slowly increased. I should have never agreed to this. What was I thinking? I wasn't cut out for this kind of stress. Maybe I could find a different job in accounting. More safe and secure.

My body jumped back into reality as the power came back on. The lights softened once more, lowering the heat coursing through my veins.

I moved forward and put my hands firmly around the microphone. "Tom, I think it's time to update your electrical system." The crowd applauded and a warm pool of light enfolded me. The music started—this time the sound system welcomed my voice.

I opened with Julie London's rendition of *Cry Me A River*. I hit each note with ease. The sound from the audience softened. Conversations muted—I had them with me all the way. Every song motivated me, and I moved to the rhythm. When I sang *Look At Me,* I made eye contact with Jerard. He leaned into the café table; his smile and eyes never left mine. I finished the hour-long show with *Come Rain or Come Shine.*

At the song's end the audience rose to their feet and clapped. They shouted, "Great job!" and "Encore!"

I didn't want this night to end. I could have gone on for another hour. I'd prepared for this moment and now it came true. What if I'd never committed to this performance? I would have never experienced this incredible adrenaline spike. I stood taller, adding another two inches to my five-foot-eleven height.

The lights went up and I made a small bow from the waist. I had to admit, I practiced several times this afternoon. After the applause died down, I stepped up again to the mic. "I would like to thank Mrs. Campbell who spent the last three years coaching me. Please take a well-deserved bow." She rose and the audience cheered. Since I arranged to have a special table set up for her and her husband, dinner was on me.

Tom came back onto the stage and hugged me. "I knew it. You were fantastic." He spoke to the crowd. "Make sure you check the newspaper for performance dates, because Sarah will be here as many weekends as I can keep her. I have a feeling this is just the beginning of a very successful career." He escorted me through the spectators.

I spotted two co-workers, Samantha and Everette, and thanked them for coming. "Your rendition of *Cry Me a River* brought me to tears," Everette said. "Are you going to have a CD out soon?"

"I'd better give that some thought. I'm glad you both came. It means so much to see familiar faces." They moved aside as other people crowded around and told me how much they enjoyed my singing. They asked so many questions: "When is your next performance? Are you singing only at Courtney's?" One couple asked for my autograph, saying they knew I was going to be a huge hit. They handed me a pen. I was actually signing my name on a paper napkin. Was this real?

Tom waltzed me over to my friends' table and I heard him ask, "What do you guys think?" He grasped his hands together as if he had watched his daughter graduate from high school.

The group all spoke at once as they sat back down. I heard the words "Great!" and "Unbelievable!"

I took a seat at their table. Jerard's chair was empty; I scanned the room but did not see him. I tugged on my earlobe. Had he left without even a goodbye?

Bill asked, "Where have you been hiding that incredible voice?"

Pins and needles traveled up my arms. Customers continued to stop by with congratulations. All the conversations buzzed around my head like bees over a lavender plant. I took it in, savoring every moment.

Someone placed their hands on my shoulders. The scent of sandalwood cologne told me who it was. I tipped my head back and he kissed my forehead. He took the seat next to mine and embraced both my hands. Jerard studied me as if photographing my face with his eyes.

He moved closer; we were the only two people in the room. "Your voice is up there with the greats like Peggy Lee and Dinah Washington. You never hesitated at reaching notes. You hit each one perfectly."

Jerard caressed my arm. His touch calmed me and I centered myself once again. I was coming down off a cloud and landing in a bed of cotton balls.

"Okay, girl." Nicole's voice startled me. "You need to pursue this. Please don't make it a one-shot deal. I want to hear more of that talent you've been hiding in your sock drawer."

I shook my head. "I was so nervous, but once I started singing, I let go and followed the music. It was so natural. We'll see where this goes."

"All that practice paid off," Liz said. "I'm so envious of your voice. I sing in the shower so only a bar of soap and a loofah can hear me." Her smile seemed relaxed.

Tom appeared behind Paul. "Just a minute, Sarah, I'll be right back." He disappeared momentarily, and came back to our table with a woman, who might be in her fifties, on his arm. She was trim and her jet-black hair was folded into a French twist. She wore a silver, low-cut cocktail dress. A pair of large, black, horn-rimmed glasses topped off her ensemble.

"Sarah, this is Lorraine Stark, owner of *The Only Jazz Club*," Tom said.

She directed her eyes at me. The rush I felt a moment ago put on its brakes. My confidence wobbled. Did she like my performance or not?

She shook my hand and took a small notebook from her purse. "I intend to steal you away from Tom and place you center stage in my club. Your voice is a mix of jazz from the Forties, but the quality shows your style — I have to say it's unique. You own it."

My face warmed. "Thank you." Somehow I couldn't come up with anything clever to say.

The waiter brought over a tray of brandy snifters.

"If anyone can promote your career, it's Lorraine." Tom placed a bottle of Cognac on the table. "A toast to you, Sarah. I'm not eager about sharing you with Lorraine, but there's no stopping you now." We raised our glasses, and as they tinkled together, my world shifted in a new direction.

Lorraine tore out a piece of paper from her notebook

and handed it to me. "Hope you don't mind, but I took some notes during your performance."

"Not at all. I'd love to hear anything you have to say." Was this really happening? Was it going too fast?

"I'll set an appointment for you with my dress designer, and we need to show off that beautiful long red hair. *You* have the talent, but *I* have the eye for design."

Tom chimed in. "Don't forget, Lorraine, I have her performing a couple of weekends here."

"I know." She handed me her card. "Call me next week and we can start working on your career. Good night, Sarah. It was a delight to hear you sing. I'll be back." Without another word she evaporated into the crowd.

I made a quick replay of the conversation. I wasn't dreaming. My life was about to take a big shift. I had done it. I knew then to follow whatever direction my career took me. I let out a small yelp.

Though my watch said 9:30 p.m., I was hardly exhausted. My energy glided along.

I crossed over to Tom, deep in conversation with Nicole and Bill, and I slid my arm around his shoulder. "Thank you, Tom, for encouraging me to take a chance." He drew me close for a big brother hug.

I was captivated, taking in all the faces of those who listened to my performance. I paused and eyed a man reclining against a wall near the entrance.

I squinted and placed a hand over my eyes to block the glare. *Oh, crap.* I'd recognize that pose anywhere. Arms crossed over his chest and that smug, overly confident smile. *Why the hell are you here, Sam?* As our eyes met, his hands brushed together in a small clap, clap. Was I supposed to be thrilled by his presence? Was he still with the twenty-one-year-old art student, or had he moved onto his next victim? It was nice not to give a rat's ass anymore. I lifted my chin and turned my back to him. Maybe he'd take the hint to get lost. He was no longer allowed to steal my confidence.

Midnight closed in and we continued huddling around our cabaret table, discussing my newfound career. I didn't want the evening to end. When Paul checked the time we'd been chatting for more than two hours

"Sorry, gang," he said, "I'm working overtime this weekend. Sarah, when you delivered *Come Rain or Come Shine* at the end of your set, I was blown away." Paul took my hand and held it. "You need to follow through with this singing. You know me. I don't give out compliments often, but tonight, well, you have a voice that should be heard."

Liz said, "Take those kudos and run with them. He rarely gives them." She rose out of her chair as did Paul, Nicole, and Bill.

"I have to get ready for an exhibit Monday," Nicole said. "So we're going to take off. I'll give you a call tomorrow. Sarah, I don't know what to say. Your voice is—it's beautiful." She set her hand on my shoulder.

The two couples headed for the door. The sound of clinking ice cubes and bar chatter had quieted. Only a few customers remained.

It was 12:15 a.m. Jerard and I continued to sit at the table.

He tugged his earlobe and his eyes lit with a twinkle of mischief. "Listen, could you come over to my place and keep this celebration going? I have a great selection of jazz and blues CDs I'd like to share. What's that old saying? 'Why don't you come up and I'll show you my art collection?'"

"I'd love that. I think I'm going to be up all night." A short film played in my mind. I imagined waking up in his bed with silk sheets covering our lower bodies.

"Let me give Tom a quick goodbye and then we can be on our way." Before I headed for Tom I turned back and kissed Jerard's cheek. "Thank you for being here tonight."

He circled his hand around my waist and delivered a slow kiss, teasing me with his tongue. I ached with the need to touch and explore every inch of his body. After the embrace I took in all the features of his face.

There was something else I had to do. *Oh – Tom.*

I found him at the cash register.

"I'm leaving," I said. "I owe you for encouraging me to get up on that stage."

"You're welcome. Glad to be of service." He mimicked a salute.

I grinned. "I'll call you in a couple of days to see if you still want me to sing Saturday night."

"You better be here next Saturday. Lorraine's going to snatch you up, so I'm going to get as much as possible out of your voice."

I returned the salute. "Yes, sir." We shared a brief hug before one of the waiters called him over.

Jerard came up behind me, turned me around, and lured me in for a long, well-earned kiss. His hand drifted down my dress, brushing my breast. Decision made—it was his place. How fast could he call for the car, unlock the door to his apartment, and rip every piece of clothing off my body?

19

CHAPTER

We proceeded out onto the curb. The crisp, cool air brought new energy to my body. Market Street was quiet except for a few late-running busses. It must have rained because the streetlight reflections bounced off the dark, wet asphalt. A few minutes later, Joe met us dressed in his usual black suit and white, button-down collar shirt. "Ma'am, I snuck in for a few minutes and heard you sing. Are you going to do another performance? I'd like to listen to the whole set next time."

Why did he feel he had to sneak in?

"I'm singing again next weekend. I'll have a seat reserved for you and a guest."

"Probably just me." He placed his hand on the car door, and I could not help feeling a little sorry for him. Maybe he was going through the same loneliness I faced for a year after Sam left. I was tempted to ask Nicole to work her blind-date magic. I'd have to think that one over.

"It's getting cold out here," Jerard said. "Let's get in the car."

"Sorry, sir," Joe said.

We welcomed the warm interior. "You know, Jerard, you were kind of short with Joe. He seems like a nice guy." I jabbed his arm while feeling more assertive for some reason.

"I just want to have you all for myself. I'm selfish that way." He raised my chin with his fingertips and brushed his lips against mine.

Oh boy, you can have as much of me as you want. I nuzzled into his neck. *By all means, be selfish.* I was going to take all the pampering I could get tonight.

We arrived at his apartment on Nob Hill around 1:30 a.m. The front of the building was lined with manicured boxwood hedges. Fuchsia-filled baskets hung at the entrance to the lobby. We rode the elevator to the eighth floor, and the glass doors revealed a vision straight out of *Architectural Digest*. White overstuffed sofas filled the front room. The room was more formal than my taste, and there was no mistaking the strong undertone of male sexuality with its chrome coffee table and lamps.

"This is incredible. An elevator that opens right into your apartment." I tucked a few loose strands of hair behind my ear. I was in a completely different world. Mine was more architectural Shabby Chic.

Jerard took my hand. "It's not mine—I just lease." He

led me over to a bay window that took up the entire length of my apartment.

My breath stalled. "I imagine sunset and sunrise are incredible."

"I'd love to show you both." He raised an eyebrow. "I'll be right back. Continue to enjoy the view."

I turned around and watched him disappear into what might be the kitchen. I'd have him give me the complete tour before the night ended.

I took in the view of the Golden Gate Bridge and San Francisco Bay. The sparkling lights reminded me of Tinker Bell spreading pixie dust. If I didn't remove my two-inch heels, my purple toe would lodge a formal complaint to the Board of Health. I stripped off the shoes and let my feet relax into the soft carpet fibers.

I watched Jerard's reflection in the window as he approached, holding two glasses. "May I just stay here for a week or two?" I was a little embarrassed by what I said. "I mean, I've never seen the bridge and the bay from this angle. The only word I can think of is exquisite. There's no other way to describe the beauty of this city."

He placed the glasses on a small side table. "Yes, it is." He came up behind me and tucked my hair to the side. "Breathtaking." He kissed my neck, and the view of the bay and bridge vanished. I closed my eyes and clung to the warmth of his lips on my skin.

Once he released me, he handed me a crystal tulip flute bubbling with golden champagne.

"To you, Sarah." The sound of the clinking glasses ignited the fire between us.

The champagne slid down my throat. If he thought he had to coax me into having two or three more glasses of this fantastic liquid to have sex with him, he was mistaken. I wanted to be clearheaded and savor each moment that his hands explored every part of me.

He took my glass and placed it alongside his on the table. "When you sang tonight, you had my soul in the palm of your hand." He unlatched my hairclip and loosened my hair. His fingers raised my Irish red strands and let them go. He placed the clip on the arm of the sofa. He took his time while a dizzying current raced up my body. My hair drifted down my back, giving me a sense of freedom.

He said, "I have a passion for jazz and blues, especially female vocalists. Your voice is right up there with Julie London and Sarah Vaughan. Tell me you're planning a career. Share your voice, quit your job, go on tour. You're that good." His focus drifted away from my eyes, passed my shoulders, and paused at my breasts.

A delicious shudder traveled within me. "I have Tom to thank for encouraging me to take the leap."

"Tom, owner of the restaurant?" Jerard's voice sounded strained.

"Yes. We've known each other since college, and he used to listen to me sing in a band. He started college late, at twenty-seven. We were both business majors. Singing was just a hobby and I quit when I got my grown-up job working at the Hollister, Wilkin, and Zephyr accounting firm downtown." I shrugged.

He clasped my hand. "So, is Tom more than a friend? Are you dating—anyone—at the moment?"

A tiny Irish jig pranced around my insides. Was he jealous?

"No. We tried dating a couple of times, but soon realized there was no chemistry, at least none on my side. We found something much more important, friendship."

"Well, I hope you'll always remain true friends." His arms drew me closer.

My heart rate increased and my body heat escalated. A light headiness took over as I anticipated what he had in mind. It was easy to lose my balance with this man. His fingertips journeyed over my shoulders and down my arms. He moved in so close his breath fanned my face. His mouth skimmed my lips with the lightest touch, seeming to devour me, and then his tongue coaxed them open. With an eager response I placed my arms around his neck, encouraging him to go deeper.

I laced my fingers through his thick, wavy black hair. He elevated a strap of my dress, letting it drift down, exposing my breast. His tongue circled my nipple, and my breathing stopped and started several times. He slid off the other strap; the silk spiraled downward and landed in a pool around my feet.

His hands moved down my spine. It was as if we were wet clay molded into one sculpture. His mouth moved to the hollow of my neck and he spun my body around. His hand swept my hair to the side, and his soft lips met my skin. My body arched and floated upward. He slid his hand between my legs; he must have felt my damp response. I was beyond ready.

"Am I moving too fast?" He whispered into my hair.

"Don't you dare stop." The words rushed out of my mouth like water crashing through concrete.

I eased out of the dress and this time I took control. I wrestled the sweater over his head, unbuttoned his shirt, and swept it to the side. I placed my hands on his chest and moved them down to his waist. My fingers quickened as I unbuckled his belt and slid down the zipper of his pants. My hand moved around him, and he drew in a deep breath. His kiss emptied my mind of all worries and concerns.

He journeyed from my neck to each breast with a light, deft touch of his lips. Then he knelt to slide my lace underwear down my legs and off my feet. His hands covered my buttocks as he eased me toward him. My legs parted and his tongue took a tour of me that made my knees loosen. My fingers were buried in his hair, and I urged him to keep going. He rose and kissed me with urgency. His hand glided down, taking my wrist, then leading me into what I hoped was the bedroom. A song from Etta James popped into my head. "At last, my love has come along. My lonely life has ended, and life is like a song."

20
CHAPTER

A few hours later I woke up next to Jerard and listened to his soft snore. A strand of hair fell over his eyes. The rays from the streetlights drifted through a small opening in the drapes and highlighted his rich olive skin. I could hear the faint pre-dawn sounds of cars and buses. If only I could stay here in bed with this man who brought my body back to life last night, but I had to get home and relieve my dog sitters.

After I heard the rustle of sheets, Jerard sat up, combing his fingers through his hair.

I pushed off the covers and my feet met the soft carpet.

His arms enveloped my waist. "Where do you think you're going?" His voice filled with early morning huskiness.

I wasn't sure where I—where *this*—was going. The night was perfect, but now I wasn't sure if this moved too fast. Why was I fighting it? Insecurities entered my head. "I have to get home and pick up my dogs. Should have been home a long time ago."

"Your dogs will be fine. *I* need the attention." His arms invited me back to bed. "I don't want to let go of you." He explored my body, kissing all the points that brought me so much pleasure. He rose up on his arms and slid into me. This time his rhythm slowed. *We're together on this journey.* My hands gathered him in so tight that our bodies melded together. He took his time, thrusting in and out.

A pleasure-filled shiver resulted in an overflow of warmth. He moved his body faster and faster, and then I heard his breath let go, and his chest melted into mine. After a few moments he rose up on his elbows, and his eyes never left me. "You're beautiful, Sarah." He skimmed his lips across my forehead, then my cheek, and placed the gentlest kiss on my lips.

He slid over on his side, never letting go of me. His fingers traveled slowly between my legs and then they moved in a slow rhythm and increased, driving me to a high that held me in a feeling of suspension. My back arched and I ascended into a climax. I touched his soft olive-colored skin. My eyes were half closed. Falling back to sleep with him would be the perfect ending.

"Can I convince you to stay for breakfast?" He tickled my side.

"I think you can convince me to do anything right now." I sat up on one elbow, running my hand down his chest, smoothing the light layer of hair.

"Be careful, I might keep you prisoner here all day." He folded me on top of him.

I wanted that more than anything—to make love, hold each other, have breakfast. What would be so wrong about that? I was afraid of being hurt, but there was a sincerity about Jerard that made me want to test the waters of trust. I wasn't going to give up. We could take it slow.

"As much as I'd like to stay, I really do need to get home." The bedside clock read 5:30 a.m. I kissed him once more before I slid out of the wonderful silk sheets.

I opened the bedroom door and gathered my clothes which were strewn all over the front room floor. Jerard tugged on his boxer shorts. He sauntered out of the bedroom and came over to me. His kisses started at my neck and journeyed down to my breasts.

I clutched my clothes in one hand. "I have to go, or I'll have two angry dachshunds staring me down."

The corners of his mouth curled upward. "I'm going to have to meet those two someday. It's a bit early to call Joe, so I'll get a cab. We can ride back to your place. I wouldn't feel right sending you home alone. Maybe we could make out in the back seat like horny teenagers."

How could I refuse? "Okay, let me get dressed and freshen up." I used his bathroom to dress but failed to do something with my face and hair. That would have to wait until I got home. I searched his medicine cabinet and found a bottle of mouthwash for a quick rinse. Afterward, I entered the front room for one last glance at the view. I could just make out the top of the Golden

Gate Bridge as the sun started to come up. The remainder was covered with fog. The city was peaceful on Sunday morning, and a few people were out with their dogs.

Wandering around I saw a desk in the corner stacked with papers and CDs. A box of chocolate-covered cherries rested atop the clutter. He said he had a sweet tooth. I remembered when he ordered peach cobbler at Courtney's.

Jerard's footsteps came up behind me. "Ready to go?"

"Oh, sure."

The cab rolled up a minute later. I enjoyed the backseat cuddling. I had almost drifted to sleep when the cab slowed in front of my apartment. Jerard transported me safely to my front porch. His fingers traversed through my hair, and his lips returned for one all-consuming kiss.

I didn't want this to end. What did I know about this man? Had I been so sexually deprived that I wanted to jump into another relationship? Was he going to be like Sam, nice and thoughtful in the beginning and then a selfish bastard in the end? Those questions spun in my head.

He stepped back, continuing to hold me. "I have to drive to Half Moon Bay tomorrow and meet with a client at her art gallery," he said. "I should return by seven o'clock. I'll call when I get back."

"Don't keep me dangling, or I'll cut off future privileges." I punched his arm lightly.

"Sounds like your last relationship left you with a few trust issues."

"You could say that. I'm working on not putting up with liars and cheats," I said.

"Sorry to hear that. You deserve better." He brushed my cheek with the back of his hand. "I give you my Eagle Scout promise, I'll call you the minute I get back." After he kissed me I watched his sexy posterior descend the stairs.

21
CHAPTER

It was almost 6:30 a.m. I considered going across to Ackermanns' to pick up Max and Gracey, but decided it was too early. I set the alarm for 8:00 a.m., and I drifted off with thoughts of Jerard lowering me onto his bed.

The alarm went off, so I threw on my robe and popped across the hall.

Mrs. Ackermann answered the door. She wore orange juice cans as hair rollers. How the hell did she sleep in those things? Mr. Ackermann appeared behind her, rubbing sleep from his eyes.

I said, "Sorry about staying out all night. Hope the dogs weren't too much trouble."

"Oh, Honey," Mr. Ackermann said, a squirming Gracey in his arms. "We love these little guys."

"Did you have a good time with your gentleman caller?" Mrs. Ackermann tried to catch a loose can sliding from her hair.

I sensed my cheeks growing hot. "Yes," I said and left it at that. "Thanks again, you two." Max came running toward me, a mouth full of milk bone. "Okay, let's go home." I waved goodbye and the two dogs trailed me across the hall.

I made a cup of coffee and went through the morning pattern with the dogs. I was getting ready to step into the shower when the phone rang and caller I.D. lit up: *Liz.*

"Hey girl, how was your evening? I want details," she said.

"Just getting into the shower. How about we meet for lunch?" I could hear Paul in the background grinding coffee beans. "I'd like to shop for a couple of dresses. If I'm going to make my singing a new career, I'll have to build some kind of performance wardrobe. How about we meet at Gino's Deli on Maiden Lane?"

"Sounds good. Let's meet around noon."

"I'll call Nicole and see if she wants to join us. That way, I don't have to recap my evening with Jerard twice."

"Okay, can't wait." She hung up.

I called Nicole and she picked up on the first ring. "Hey, Sarah, let's not waste time—I want to know about your night with Jerard."

"Listen, how about you join Liz and me at Gino's Deli around noon? I'll fill you in on all the details."

"Sure. Did you see the pictures of those murdered women on today's front page?" Nicole asked.

"I haven't read the paper yet."

"Bill decided to hire a security guard whenever I'm working at a gallery. Imagine that. This whole thing is creepy, isn't it?"

"Frightening would be the word I'd use. You be careful." We hung up. I did not want to upset her or Bill by telling them I saw the dead girl in the park. I would find a better time.

I finished my Sunday chores and opted for a cab instead of the bus to meet the girls. I arrived at the restaurant at noon. Gino's had a cafeteria-style set up, and the light crowd on Sunday made it perfect for a quick lunch. The automatic glass door opened to the sound of people ordering food, plates hitting trays, and shared conversations. The smell of hot pastrami, San Francisco sourdough bread, and homemade soup increased my appetite.

The girls waited for me inside. I greeted them with a short embrace before focusing my attention on the daily specials scratched on the blackboard behind the counter. I decided on clam chowder and a slice of sourdough bread. The bell over the door jingled and I glanced back. What? Jerard's driver, Joe? He raised his hand. Since he was dressed in jeans and a sweatshirt, I guessed it was his day off.

"Hey, Joe," I called out. "This is a coincidence." I lifted my eyebrows.

"Yeah, I've only lived in the city for a couple of months, so I like to try different restaurants on my day off." He shifted back and forth on each leg, and a blush reddened his cheeks.

His explanation wasn't a hundred percent convincing. He tugged the sleeves of his sweatshirt.

I slid my tray down to the young cashier. "Cash or credit?" he asked.

"Cash. And add an iced tea to my order, please." I switched back to Joe. I blurted out the words without giving them much thought. "Why don't you join us after you order? We're sitting in the back corner." I pointed toward my confidantes.

"You sure?"

"Maybe you're meeting someone?"

I hoped he was. I wanted an afternoon with Liz and Nicole.

"No, just me." He stared at my friends a little too long; he made the hair tingle on the back of my neck.

"Great." His voice rose a pitch higher.

Wow. You'd think I asked him to the prom. Was he lonely?

I picked up my tray and headed to our table. I took my time clearing my food and drink off the tray. I knew Nicole and Liz would drill me about Jerard, and I wanted to torture them a little.

"All right, we want all the facts about last night."

Nicole clasped my arm.

I took the tray over to the back counter before joining them. "I'm giving you the condensed version because I've asked Joe to come sit with us. He's Jerard's driver. Remember him from Courtney's?"

"Yeah. Kinda weird he showed up here, don't you think?" Liz stole a look at Joe who waited for his order.

"Enough about him. Details." Nicole imitated a puppy, with paws up and tongue hanging out.

I rested my chin in my hand and closed my eyes briefly. I peeked through one eye, and as I suspected, the girls were glued at the shoulders. If I delayed a minute longer, they would pounce.

I shook my head. "Let's say Jerard made me the happiest I've been in a long time and leave it at that."

"Come on. We're two old married women. We need to spice up our dull lives." Liz slid her chair closer.

Joe approached us. "Ladies." His greeting apparently robbed Liz and Nicole of their enthusiasm. They sighed, obviously disappointed.

"You remember Liz and Nicole?" I pointed at each respectively. "This is Joe. He's Jerard's driver."

"Yes," he said, "I remember seeing you with Jerard and Sarah. How are you?"

"Fine." They answered in unison with flat voices. Nicole sipped her water, keeping her focus on Joe.

I said, "Grab a chair and sit with us." In a way I was glad he was joining our group. I could keep the more intimate details about my night with Jerard to myself.

Joe put his chair between mine and Nicole's. I let him

wedge in.

"Hope I'm not interrupting your lunch." His eyebrows rose. "I was going to see if there were any half-price theater tickets. I like going to shows, but the prices are getting so high."

"A man of surprises." Nicole said. "Do you usually go alone, or do you have a girlfriend?"

He shook his head. "Alone."

I placed my hand on his wrist. "Here it comes—watch out or Miss Matchmaker will have you set up in no time."

"Actually, I'm kind of a loner. Haven't met the right woman yet." He didn't take his eyes off Nicole. "Before I forget, I thought the mosaic table Mr. Colbert bought from you is beautiful. I was there to pick him up when it was delivered. You're very talented."

Nicole flashed her award-winning smile and went back to eating her sandwich.

What was it about Joe that made me uncomfortable? Why ever would we run into him here? Strange.

22
CHAPTER

Joe kept his eyes on Nicole as if no one else was in the room. Did she just shiver? Was he making her uncomfortable? There he went again, tugging on his sleeve. Maybe he was shy or there was something wrong with him. He sure did not have the greatest social skills.

Nicole started to cough and then a sneezing attack came on. She retrieved a package of tissues from her purse. "I hope I'm not getting a cold. I have a showing this week."

"Where is it?" His hand touched her forearm.

She squinted at his hand and he retracted it.

He said, "Sorry. It's just that the table Jerard bought made me want to see more of your work."

Nicole nodded as if she accepted his explanation. She took a long drink of water and adjusted her distance away from him.

This was a bad idea. I needed to distract him. She usually liked to be flirted with, even though she was married, but she wasn't too crazy about this guy.

"Did you say you've only lived here a couple of months?" I asked.

He hesitated, swallowing hard.

Someone's phone rang. We reached for our phones. Joe clutched the pocket of his sweatshirt, fetched his cell, and looked at the caller I.D. "I'm going to have to call this person back. I'm sure I'll be seeing a lot more of you, Sarah." He wrapped his sandwich in a napkin.

"I think you might."

He scooted his chair back. "Nicole, I'll see you at your showing. You never told me where it was."

"The Uno Gallery on Post and Taylor." Her voice fell to a whisper.

"Okay, see you there." He rested his hand on her shoulder.

And she stiffened.

Before Joe made it to the exit, his phone rang, and we heard him yell into it. "I know. Get off my back, I'll be right there." He cocked his neck to the right as if trying to get rid of tension. "Bye, Sarah," he said.

I raised my chin in acknowledgment.

"What the hell was that about?" Liz's voice broke the silence. "My God, Nicole, the guy needed a napkin to wipe off the drool."

"Yeah, it struck me as odd. He's cute in a baby-faced way, but he creeped me out. I usually like attention, but not this time. I don't want him to show up at the gallery. Don't you think he was coming on a bit too strong, Sarah?" Nicole rubbed her arms.

"A little, I guess. Not much. Hell, I don't know. You're asking someone who doesn't read men too well." I fumbled with my napkin and tossed it on the table. "On a lighter note, I plan to see where this goes with Jerard. I'm coming out of a dark cave, and I'm going to take a chance."

The light came back into the girls' eyes. They were ready for last evening's details. That was the reason for this lunch after all. I filled them in on some highlights but kept the more personal ones to myself. We finished eating and headed out to the street.

"I'll call you this week," I said. A strong wind blew, and I had to brush the hair away from my face.

"Not that it's any of my business—" Nicole took my hand. "But I think Jerard should hire another driver. I'm not comfortable with Joe being so close to you. There's something about him that screams *stay away*."

"I agree." Liz chimed in.

"I'll see how Jerard feels about him." After our group hug Liz and Nicole shared a cab home. I had a longing in my gut, so intense that tears pooled in the corners of my eyes. I wanted to go home to someone. I had Jerard in mind. *Take it slow.*

I decided to do some shopping. After an hour or so, I hadn't found anything that shouted "torch singer." I

141

took my time going up Geary Street and reading the posters about an upcoming performance of *Death of a Salesman*. Was Joe able to purchase a half-price ticket? There was something off about him. I didn't like the way he touched Nicole—too familiar. I shook those thoughts out of my head. Those murdered women had me suspicious of everyone. Didn't Joe say he'd only lived here a couple of months? *Okay, stop.* I headed to the curb and flagged down a cab.

I returned home about half past four. I was hoping for that phone call from Jerard, but it never came. Tomorrow was Monday, back to the real world. I prepared my clothes for work, fed the dogs, and read for a while. It was 9 p.m. when I let the dogs out for the last time. My head hit the pillow where I had some interesting X-rated dreams about Jerard. Luckily I had no visions of dead girls.

23
CHAPTER

The alarm went off and I prepared for work. Another day off sounded tempting — I could take the pups to the beach. I thought of wet sand caressing my feet amidst the scent of ocean air — what a perfect place to relive my vocal performance. But missing work this time was not in the cards.

I turned in an advertising proposal to my boss last week, and I hoped he had good news for me today. I suggested we get our name out into the community and meet with small businesses about our firm's services. After I changed my clothes twice, I settled on a black suit with a white silk blouse and slipped on my tennis shoes. There was a pair of red heels in my purse. Max and Gracey lined up at the front door. I hooked their leashes and headed over to the Ackermanns' apartment.

I caught the bus on Mission Street and arrived thirty minutes later at the Hollister, Wilken, and Zephyr office at Washington and Montgomery Streets, known as the "Wall Street of the West."

I'd spent the last five years working for this firm. My proposal offered a chance to boost my career in a new direction. "Today's the day," I muttered. "He's going to love my ideas, and I'll have the change I've been wanting." At my stop, I headed off the bus and tightened my coat collar. The wind howled between buildings, giving me a haunting sensation. I arrived at my building and shoved the door open. A gust rustled the front of my skirt.

I joined the herd of employees emptying out of the street and into their offices. We switched our direction from the out-of-order elevator to the staircase. The cattle drive aimed upward, and we peeled off to our designated corrals.

My tennis shoes carried me up the stairs to the tenth floor. Once I passed through the office door, I heard the symphony of conversations, computers humming, and printers drinking ink at a rapid speed. Although I wanted change, I also felt comfort in coming to work and seeing familiar faces. I had grown used to this weekly pattern—it fit me like a pair of well-broken-in sandals.

I almost arrived at my desk when someone shouted, "Hey, Sarah." Everette's back pressed against the wall next to the water cooler where most of us caught up on our daily lives. He had that fresh-out-of-college spirit. Blond bangs draped over his forehead, rosy cheeks highlighted his skin, and his smile captured several women's attention in the office. He had asked me out every week for about two months, and I let him down with my old stand-by, "Everette, I'm getting out of a bad relationship and not ready to date."

He was a wonderful person, but his flame didn't ignite my pilot light. I convinced him to ask out Samantha, a co-worker who nabbed her inhaler every time he passed by. Now the two of them were in each other's pockets.

"Samantha and I loved your performance Saturday." He placed his hand against his chest. "We're bringing two more couples with us next weekend. I wracked my brain out trying to figure who you sounded like. No one. Your voice is unique."

"Thanks." My face heated up. I had a fan club.

I ducked into my synthetic, seven-by-seven-foot cubicle, dropped into my chair, and spun around. Instead of an assistant accountant, I was now a torch singer.

I yanked on the bottom drawer, tossed in my tennis shoes, and shoved my feet into my red power heels. I met with my first client who was close to retirement. He kept all his books manually. I tried to convince him to change over to the computer, but it wasn't going to happen.

My second client was meticulous when it came to details. Her books were all organized on the computer, line items skillfully entered. I was as proud of her as a mom who viewed her child's first straight-A report card. I finished some paperwork and noticed it was 11:00 a.m.

"Ms. Soon." Fred, my boss's assistant, popped around my cubicle into my workspace. "Mr. Shaffer would like to speak to you." He straightened his tie.

I had a strong feeling this would be about my proposal. I was going to try to convince Shaffer to update our ads. We needed to connect with new and upcoming businesses in the city because we had clients who brought us black ledgers with all numbers entered by hand.

Fred's annoying voice interrupted my thoughts. "I hear the company's making some cuts. Hope it's not bad news." He did a half-spin on his grandiose heel and headed back to his desk.

Well, thank you so much, Fred. What an ass. I shook my head and aimed my thoughts at my proposal. My expertise was accounting, but I wanted to branch out into advertising. If this outdated company was going to stay in business, it would have to move forward. We needed clients who were not afraid of change. *Listen to me, the one who fears change the most. No, today I'm going to sell this, and he's going to buy.*

I tugged the hem of my blazer and straightened my skirt. The hallway to Mr. Shaffer's office seemed longer today. His secretary Jennifer peered up from her computer as I passed her desk. She started straightening papers which did not appear to need straightening. *Something's wrong. No — stay positive.*

I tapped on my boss's glass door. He was on the phone and signaled me in to take a seat. I shut the door and sat down. I observed the photo of his wife with their two kids on his desktop. I read the awards displayed on the wall behind him. *Get off the phone.* The anticipation was killing me.

My stomach quivered—Fred's annoying words popped back into my head. Was this about my proposal or my job? I adjusted my posture and pumped confidence back into my veins. Mr. Shaffer ended his call and placed his elbows on the desk. When I started here five years ago, he'd appeared young and had the energy of a three-hundred-watt light bulb. Today his shoulders slumped and he had more gray hair.

His eyes dulled and his usual boyish grin was nowhere in sight. "Ms. Soon." I picked up the unease in his shaky voice. He let out a loud breath as he shoved the open file in front of him. I saw my photo paper-clipped to the upper left side. He clasped his hands together, rubbed his chin a couple of times, and eyed the folder again.

I nodded. That's *my* name. "Mr. Shaffer." I sat on an alarm clock ready to go off. Was he going to accept my ideas or not? I couldn't stand the thought of continuing this tedium year after year. If he didn't accept it, would I start preparing myself for a new job? Beads of sweat formed on my upper lip, and I dabbed them with the side of my hand.

He continued to read my file and fingered the edge of the paper. "It says here that you've been with our company for five years."

"Yes," I said. Where was this going?

"Our clients have given you excellent reviews. Your accuracy is impeccable and they all mention how comfortable you make them feel during meetings. Your coworkers always comment on how quick you are to help if they need assistance." He tugged an earlobe.

"Mr. Shaffer, I worked so hard on that proposal. What is it that you don't like? Maybe we can go over it together and make any needed changes." I slid my chair closer to the edge of his desk. The toe of my left foot wiggled.

"It's not about the proposal. I agree with a lot of what you included. We do need to put more effort in marketing and connecting with our community. I was particularly drawn to your idea of skilled computer techs and updating our formats. But this is about your position. Due to cutbacks, I'm going to have to give you two weeks' notice, with severance pay of course." He combed his hands through his hair.

"What? I'm being laid off?" My heart dropped to my stomach.

He exhaled and scraped his hand over his face. Then he thrust back his chair and paced over to the window.

"Anything I can do to keep my job? I can work extra hours, take on more clients." I joined him at the window. "You need to pay attention to me."

He backed away from me.

I continued. "This isn't fair." Heat flushed through my body. "You just said I was doing a great job here, my co-workers had positive things to say about me. You even liked my proposal. How can you say these things and then let me go?" I threw my arms up in the air, and he retreated toward his desk. Then he closed my file.

My hands gripped the edge of his desk. "That's it? Just like that? You close my file and I'm gone? I can't afford to lose this job." My voice verged on begging. All my earlier confidence had been vacuumed up. "Did I do something wrong?"

"No, you didn't. That's why this is so difficult. You're not the only one losing a job. I have to let three other people go. I fought to keep you on, but money's tight, and employees with five years or less are the first to go. I'm so sorry." He plopped back into his chair. "I hope the severance pay will carry you through until you find another job, Sarah."

He'd never called me Sarah before. I crossed my arms. "I guess there's nothing I can say or do. I don't think I want to stick around for two weeks. I'll have to get out there and see if there are any jobs available. Who do I see about receiving my severance pay?"

"I'll contact payroll and it will be mailed to you in two weeks." He fidgeted with my folder and rotated his wrist to check the time.

"Thanks for trying to keep me on." I backed away from his desk.

"Of course."

I guessed my time was up. He must have been hoping

I'd leave his office quickly. "I'd appreciate it if you would write that letter of recommendation."

"No problem." He picked up the phone.

I could take the hint, meeting was over. I left his office. *That's it, five years and thanks a lot.* A painful lump rose in my throat.

24

CHAPTER

During the journey back to my desk, I felt a few eyes watching as I passed by. Did they know I was being laid off? Fred came out of his cubicle but backed up when he saw the deflated energy in my face.

"Everything okay?" He asked as if he didn't know.

"No. Everything's *not* okay." I whispered "asshole" under my breath and headed to my desk. I sat there for a while taking in the top of my desk decorated with a photo of Gracey and Max, a coffee cup with a chipped rim, and a stack of client folders.

What should I do with the folders? Should I call my clients? This morning I was on top of the world. My singing performance and my night with Jerard. Now I had no job. I opened the bottom drawer and removed my tennis shoes and a pair of black heels.

The chipped coffee cup was a gift from my aunt the

first day I came to work. It had bold letters on it: *Accountants Rule.* I threw the fancy shoes back in the drawer. *Who needs heels when you're unemployed?* I picked up the plant with one green leaf remaining and threw it into the trash. My toes wiggled again inside my red power shoes. *A lot of good you did.* I replaced them with tennis shoes and crammed the red ones into my briefcase.

What was I going to do? I had the money my aunt left me, so I could get by for about three months. I sagged into my chair and panic invaded my thoughts. My job was like my family. I would have to redo my resume. Who was hiring? If this company was laying off people, maybe there were no other accounting jobs available. I grabbed a handful of my hair and yanked hard. *Don't let anyone see you cry.* Too late — tears spilled over and streamed down my cheek.

I heard Everette say my name. I tried to wipe away the tears before he saw them, but I wasn't quick enough. "Why are you crying? Did Shaffer turn down the proposal?" He bent down and covered my hands with his.

"No, I was laid off." I could not stop the waterworks.

"What, why? You're the best accountant in the office. What the hell?" He rose in the direction of Shaffer's office.

"He said they're cutting costs, and anyone with less than five years has to go." How long had Everette been working here?

"Great. Guess I'll be next." He perched on the edge of my desk.

"Maybe not. He said he had three more layoffs. Hopefully, you won't be one of them. He gave me two weeks, but I'm leaving now. I have to find another job. Do you know of anyone hiring?" My voice cracked.

"No, but I'll start checking around. God, this is awful." His brows edged together—he must be nervous about his own security.

"I need to finish packing. I'm really going to miss coming to work. You're such a good friend."

He held out his arms in a welcome embrace. "Don't worry, you'll find a job and don't forget, we'll be back to hear you sing."

He left me with nothing to do but throw things in a box. I covered the coffee cup with an old newspaper. *Accountants Rule? Not this one, not today.*

After five years here, I didn't even have enough stuff to fill this cardboard piece of shit. Instead I unpacked it, shoved the photo and mug in my purse, and hurled the empty box across the cubicle. I seized the coat off the back of my chair and headed for the exit. Fellow employees remained glued to their computers as I took my last pass through these halls. I elbowed the door open and headed out. Who would be next to pack up their things?

25
CHAPTER

My watch read 12:10 p.m. The lunch crowd huddled around the elevator I nicknamed "the metal dragon." It swallowed you up then spit you out at the end of the day. The dragon seized me one last time.

While descending to the ground floor, I studied the faces of those crammed in with me. If I told them I just got laid off, would they care? I barely knew any of the people who entered this building daily.

I should have made more friends, gone out to lunch more with coworkers. Should have, could have. What was the use? My hands shook and I felt claustrophobic in the elevator. Why was it taking so long to get to the first floor? I tried to wriggle my way forward, but there was nowhere to go. Finally, the doors parted and I leaped out. My head was spinning—was I going to throw up?

I made it to the lobby door without passing out. I exited the building, knowing this would be the last time. The damp, ice-cold air gripped me as the door swung shut behind me. I took one last glimpse at the building I'd entered five days a week for five years. *Goodbye, paycheck.*

I traversed Montgomery Street, turning up Post and down to Union Square where I stood in front of Sid's Café. Someone bumped me and sent a shock wave through my body. My arms clutched my sides as if to hold them together. My purse and briefcase collided, and one of my red shoes fell to the ground. While bending to pick it up, I considered throwing the pair in the garbage, but I changed my mind and shoved the shoe back in my purse.

Maybe I should have given Liz a call, but her hands were full preparing a fundraiser for the Children's Center. I tried Nicole and the recording went to message. What would I say? *Hello, Nicole, I just lost my job. In three months, I won't be able to pay my rent. Other than that, I'm fine.* I hung up without a word.

I was off-balance, so I went into Sid's for a cup of coffee and something to eat. Though the café was packed with the lunch crowd, most of them gainfully employed, I managed to secure a counter stool where I had a view onto Union Square.

The aroma of pastrami and onion rings wafted from the kitchen. Normally I would order that plate every couple of weeks, but today the smell nauseated me. I heard fresh coffee beans being ground and watched baristas work their magic. *Anyone else out there lose their job today?* I wanted to shout.

The conversation in my head bantered back and forth. I scanned the customers in the restaurant who laughed, gossiped, and shook hands. Their world kept spinning while mine was shattered. I tugged at a chipped fingernail so hard it started to bleed. I removed a napkin from the holder and dabbed it against yet another injury for the day.

I crumpled my napkin and took in the tourists wandering the square. A couple scrutinized a fold-up map, holding it tight as the wind wrestled with its edges. Kitty-corner from the café, I spotted the half-price theater ticket office where a line of customers snaked around the square. Bundled in scarves, heavy coats, and hats, they fought to keep out the chill. The sun disappeared behind black clouds.

Someone appeared at my side, and I nearly tumbled off my stool. "Hey, I didn't mean to startle you." Brenda, my favorite waitress, smiled down at me, her order pad and pencil in hand. She flipped her blonde ponytail off her shoulder.

"Hi." I did my best to produce a weak grin.

"Bad day?" She bit down on the end of her pencil.

"Yeah. Just got laid off."

"Coffee's on me. I'll be right back." She darted over to the espresso machine, and a few minutes later returned, carrying a latte topped with a cream heart.

"Brenda, you just lifted my spirits. But I don't have

much of an appetite after what happened. Think I'll just have a small chef salad."

"You got it, girl." She stuck the pencil behind her ear and headed to another table.

The heart melted into the coffee. There was a thickness in my throat, but no tears. A couple of days ago, I was high on my singing performance adrenaline, but today — zap! — Mr. Shaffer had ripped the euphoria right out from under me.

When I lost my parents and my aunt and uncle, I had experienced the same hollow feeling. Alone. If I sat here forever, I would not have to face the facts — I had no job to go to tomorrow, no chit-chat by the water cooler, no discussion of a recent movie.

Brenda's arm crossed my vision and she placed the now-unwanted salad in front of me. The lettuce was as wilted as I was.

"Listen, Sarah, something better's going to come along. I'm a firm believer." She rested her hand on my shoulder for several seconds. I placed my hand over hers, offering a silent thank you.

I scooted the lettuce around my plate, took one bite with my fork, and let it drop to the counter. Something stuck in my throat, so I took a sip of lukewarm coffee to wash it down.

My mind wandered around the world and back. It dropped me off in Jerard's apartment. His hands searched every part of my body. I replayed our love scene over and over as if it were an Art Nouveau movie. He said he would be out of town today, something about Half Moon Bay. I wished I were back in his bed under warm blankets, his strong arms holding me, making everything better.

The crowd dwindled, leaving only a few customers in the café. I hadn't realized how much time had passed. I had been sitting for more than an hour, but I had to clean up my resume and find another job. I peered at my uneaten salad and stabbed a piece of lettuce. As my fork headed toward my mouth, a familiar shape outside the window distracted me.

A man wearing a fedora strode at a determined pace through Union Square. He stopped in the center to tighten his coat collar. I narrowed my eyes and squinted. That's when I recognized his bronze, chiseled profile.

Jerard!

Should I run out and shout "hello?" No. Something was kicking up inside me. I ran through the recent things he told me. There it was. He said he would be in Half Moon Bay all day. My breath quickened and the knot returned to my stomach. First Sam and now him? Was he just another liar in my life?

A flood of self-doubt poured out. I slipped off the stool, put on my coat, left a generous tip, and deserted my half-eaten salad. I headed out the door. *Follow him, confront him. Find out what kind of lies he creates.* This day just got better and better.

What started as a light rain turned into a downpour as people scattered for shelter. Umbrellas popped opened all around me—I could not see Jerard. Finally, I spotted him heading over to the corner of Powell and Post streets. *You have some explaining to do and I'm not in the mood for any bullshit.* I headed in his direction.

26
CHAPTER

I stood behind a kiosk, then peeped around to watch him. The rain came down so hard I had to wipe drops from my eyes. He seemed to ignore the blinking "no walk" sign, barely making it across Post Street.

After he dodged a couple of cabs, one of the drivers yelled out the window, "Hey, idiot!" Jerard raised his arms as if to apologize. His pace accelerated and he collided with an elderly man. He placed one hand on the man's shoulders to steady him, but the man whacked him with his cane.

What are you up to?

His pace picked up again. I dodged a group of tourists. I was soaked and my tennis shoes made squeaking sounds. He crossed Sutter Street and entered the Manchester Art Gallery. I did not cross after him; instead I found shelter as I ducked into the entry of a small hat shop. From there I had a full view of the art gallery. Two sculptures dominated the window along with a couple of paintings mounted on easels.

He removed his hat and shook off the raindrops. The woman who greeted him wore a cream-colored suit that melted into her curves. Her hair was brown and shoulder length. Jerard chatted with Miss Happy Hips as her hand flipped her hair. Once in a while she gave a shallow snicker.

He snatched a folder from his briefcase, placed it on the counter, and popped it open. They turned their backs to me. She was practically molded into his side. They appeared to sift through the contents.

I moved out of the shelter of the hat shop and did my best girl-private-eye impersonation as I shifted around a newspaper stand at the corner. Jerard stuck his hat back on and shook hands with Miss Happy Hips. Then she stroked his arm. She was quite touchy-feely. He glanced out the door and I ducked my head. Did he see me?

I chanced another peek—he placed the papers back in his briefcase, except for a newspaper tucked under one arm, and then he departed from the gallery. He traveled farther up Powell Street. What the hell was I doing? Was I going to follow him in the rain for hours?

I trailed Sam once, and here I was again, reliving the insanity. My hair was drenched and the damp air made me shiver. I stepped away from the newspaper stand; like some crazed woman, I continued to follow him. *You're an idiot, Sarah.*

After turning left on Bush Street, Jerard entered the Urban Art Gallery. I edged closer to the entry, then flattened my back against the window. What would I do if he saw me? Run?

I heard the man in a pinstriped suit greet him. "May I help you, sir?"

"Just browsing." He made a quick tour of the paintings on display, left his briefcase closed, and headed out the door.

I planted myself, full-frontal, right in his path as I switched from girl private eye to superhero. "Well, hello there," I said. My pulse sped up and my heart hammered against the inside of my chest.

"Sarah." He startled. The newspaper remained tucked under his arm.

I bit my lower lip. "Thought you were going to Half Moon Bay."

"Ah, I . . . ." His right hand removed the newspaper and slapped it against the side of his leg.

I had heard this hesitation from Sam. Excuses, lies. "Never mind. I don't need this. You're not going to make a fool of me. I'm done. Don't bother calling again. I'm ending this now." I spun on my heels.

"Sarah, wait—" He gripped my elbow.

I faced him, yanked my arm away, and stumbled backward. "No new excuses. I've heard them all."

Jerard's hand moved over his face; he exhaled deeply.

"Please, just listen."

"Okay, let's hear how creative you can be." I crossed my arms.

"I was a lieutenant on the Tampa, Florida Police Department. Now I'm a private investigator."

"Well, that's one I haven't heard before. So, you're not a troubleshooter for failing art galleries?"

"Wait—let me show you my ID." He was reaching for his wallet when a kid on a skateboard came barreling down Bush Street and bumped him hard. "Hey, watch where you're going," Jerard yelled.

"Sorry, dude." The kid smirked.

The half-assed apology did not sit well with Jerard. His newspaper fell to the ground near my feet. I scanned the exposed front page. There they were—photos of the five murdered women—the same ones I'd seen on TV—glaring up at me. A sixth photo appeared below them—the dead woman in the park. But in the photograph she seemed so alive and happy, ready for whatever life had in store for her.

Jerard retrieved the paper, removed his wallet from his back pocket, and flashed his private investigator ID. Pointing at the newspaper photo of the third woman across, he said, "This one, Clarissa Kazakian, was my brother's fiancée. She was murdered in Tampa, Florida two years ago, and I was the first officer on scene."

"God. I'm so sorry." I slapped my hand over my mouth. I took in a deep, painful breath and squeezed my eyes shut. I was ashamed of my behavior. I seized his hand—I couldn't think of anything else to say.

After a few silent moments, he continued. "My brother Mike is a successful lawyer in Tampa. He was so devastated he didn't go to work for about four months. I wasn't sure if he'd ever get over her loss. He became obsessed with finding Clarissa's killer. Mike knew I was doing everything I could. I must have interviewed hundreds of possible suspects.

"I asked family and friends if they were aware of anything different about Clarissa. Did she complain about someone following her? Or unwanted phone calls? I came up with very little. I started researching murders similar to Clarissa's and found a pattern. I even used my vacation time to work on the case.

"The killer used particular details. He'd place his victim against a tree and dress her in clothes that weren't hers. I read about a murder that took place near Los Angeles and contacted the LAPD.

"That murder had the same details. I decided to go out on my own as a private investigator. I had the finances to set myself up in Los Angeles. Instinct told me this was the same serial killer and I was closing in on him."

My thoughts scrambled in my head as I tried to understand everything he told me. I realized I still held his hand. "So, are you from Tampa?" The poor man just spilled his guts and I asked him to validate where he was from?

He said, "Yes, originally. I also found his other victims worked in art galleries, as did Clarissa. My brother and I came up with a plan for me to gain entry into the art world. I pretended to be an expert in improving sales. This killer has a connection to art in some way. I ran into several dead ends until I found out from LAPD that one girl had managed to escape from this monster."

"Was she able to describe him?" I rubbed my arms to get some warmth.

The wind picked up and sent the downpour sideways. He guided me deeper into the doorway.

"Her name's Karen Johnson. She was in and out of consciousness with head trauma for several months. It took her until last month to remember what happened. She doesn't know how she got away."

"That poor girl." I could not imagine her fear. I started to shake, and it was not from the sopping cold. "Where did they find her?"

"On the side of a road. We caught a break. She must have scratched him because they found blood under her nails that wasn't hers. We sent the DNA to the San Francisco crime lab over a month ago for testing. The report is ready."

"It takes that long to get DNA?"

"Yeah. Ms. Johnson agreed to meet with a sketch artist a couple days ago. The drawing will be faxed to Paul's office this evening."

"Paul knew you weren't telling the truth. He had you figured out way before I did." I shook my head.

"He's good at his job. Instead of going to Half Moon Bay, I decided to check out the art galleries here in the city."

166

My chin dipped. "Well, I feel like a fool stalking you through downtown San Francisco. I thought you were just another liar." I tucked strands of drenched hair behind my ear.

He cupped my cheek with his hand. "It's okay. You didn't know about all of this. I'm sorry I had to keep things from you. Now we hope he's in the database. I had a strong feeling he'd continue up the coast, and the murder in Golden Gate Park confirmed my thoughts. This killing was only six months after the Los Angeles one. His M.O. is changing, and he's no longer waiting a year between attacks. The interval is shortening. I just don't know—he may have left the city already."

"All of those girls—especially your brother's fiancée."

Jerard rubbed his forehead. Was he trying to erase the memory?

"Why did you feel you had to lie to me? You could have told me all of this when we met the first night at the restaurant. Why the secrecy?" I fought the chill that gripped me.

"I think you should know one more thing." He placed my hand on his chest.

"There's more?" I asked. I wasn't sure I could process any more information. My legs weakened—I needed to sit down. I rested my head on his shoulder. "How can there be anything else?"

27
CHAPTER

Jerard's forehead wrinkled and he hesitated a few seconds. "Joe's not really my driver. He's Clarissa's brother." He yanked off his fedora, brushed away the raindrops, and moved his hands through his hair.

"Wait!" My mouth dropped. "Joe's sister?" I shook my head. Had I heard correctly?

"Yeah. His sister was five years younger. They were pretty close. When Joe found out through my brother that I was going to start my own search for the killer, he joined me. He left his job, which he was going to quit anyway, and my brother put him on the payroll. He came with me to San Francisco. Joe's been renting a studio apartment on California Street. He didn't accidentally show up at your lunch with the girls—he's really keeping an eye on Nicole. When I moved here, I started visiting the art galleries and that's when I met Nicole. I was shocked at how much she resembled the murdered girls, especially Clarissa."

I didn't think Nicole resembled the women. Maybe I needed to make a closer study of the photographs.

"That's why Joe paid so much attention to Nicole at lunch. I can't imagine the pain he experienced sitting next to her." I couldn't stop the falling tears.

Jerard brushed them away with his thumb. "I did my best to spend time trying to find out as much as I could about her. I must have made an impression because she invited me to dinner to meet her husband and friends. I thought it would be a good idea for Joe to keep an eye on Nicole for extra security." He put his hat back on and secured it with a sharp tug.

"Why all the secrecy?" I searched his eyes. If only I could find an answer inside those emeralds.

Jerard revealed his next point. "I couldn't tell you because we're close to a lead on the killer."

"Does this have anything to do with the woman found in Golden Gate Park?"

"Yeah."

"I saw her, the dead woman." I put my head in my hands and rubbed hard at my eyebrows.

He snatched my elbows and drew me in close.

My adrenaline intensified.

"What? What do you mean? You *saw* her?"' He softened his grip.

"The murder happened, as you probably know, right before my singing debut. I didn't want to say anything to you. I wanted to jam it into the back of my mind."

"Tell me everything you remember, Sarah, every detail you can dig up." His face was so close I felt warm breath on my cheek.

"I met Tom in the park that day to go over my singing contract. You remember him, from Courtney's restaurant?"

"Yeah." He rolled his hand, encouraging me to continue.

"I had my dogs, Gracey and Max, with me, but Max got away and headed toward a tree inside the yellow police tape. Max grabbed the edge of the tarp that covered the murdered girl. I remember standing there, unable to move. Her skin was pale and her clothes were outdated. Her outfit was right out of a Fifties fashion magazine. A pleated skirt and a cardigan twinset, the type of clothes my mother wore."

I was in a daze as I recaptured the memory of that horror scene. I must have stopped spilling words because I heard Jerard's voice. "Do you remember any other details? Her hair, anything about her hair?" He released his grip on my elbows.

I scratched my cheek. If only I could recapture my thoughts. "There was some kind of clip or barrette holding her hair to one side."

"Shit, it's *him*."

In frustration Jerard swiped his hat off and smacked it

against the side of his leg. "I haven't been able to get all the details about the crime scene from SFPD."

A muscle tightened in my neck. "Her skin was ashen, and the crimson-red lipstick was smeared over her lips. Her throat was bruised, and I think she might have been strangled with the red scarf tied around her neck."

"What else? Do you remember anyone suspicious standing around?" He captured my shoulders and lured me close to his chest.

"No. This is the first time I've told anyone about that poor woman." I moved away and covered my mouth. When I heard Jerard's cellphone ring, I flinched.

He dropped his arms and drew the phone from his back pocket. He turned away as he spoke. "I need to meet with you. I have more information. See you in about fifteen minutes." He ended the conversation and shoved the phone back into his pants.

"Who was that?" Damn. I wasn't going to be left out of this situation.

"Paul. I called him this morning and asked if I could come down to the precinct. I let him know who I was, but he knew all along I wasn't being straightforward. I'm taking the file I've built on Clarissa over to him right now. Paul's a smart detective—he spotted me as an imposter right away.

"If Paul and I work together, maybe we can finally track down the killer. Our perp murdered two women in Savannah, but after that he committed single killings, then moved on. He's getting sloppy and, as I said before, his time frame is shrinking."

"That poor girl in the park. He killed her, didn't he?" I squeezed my hands together.

"Listen, I have to get to Paul's office. I'll call you in the morning and fill you in on details after our meeting."

I set the palm of my hand on his cheek. "Wait a minute. I have to ask you something before you go."

"Go ahead." He kept glancing up and down the street; he seemed anxious to get to his meeting.

"Was our second date a means to get closer to Nicole? Did you want to go out with me, or was this all part of the setup you and Joe planned?"

"No. Sarah, there's something between us, and I don't want to screw it up. Please believe me. After I catch this creep, my plan is to spend more time with you. Don't give up on me. I was happy that I met Nicole. Being with you that night was the best thing that'd happened to me in a very long time."

I felt his lips on mine and my feelings of hopelessness disappeared. All thoughts of the murdered woman and the loss of my job vanished. There was something special with Jerard and I did not want to let go of it.

His arms encircled me, and the cool air turned warm. *Let me stay here, don't leave.* He gently released me and raised his right hand to hail a cab. "Go home and make sure you lock those dead bolts of yours."

"Jerard," I whispered.

"Yes?" he asked.

The rain halted. I slid my hand down his arm "Thank you for being honest with me. It's been a long time since I've been able to trust a man. Even though you went about it the wrong way." I shifted a few loose hairs off his forehead. "It means a lot that you told me the truth."

He kissed me again before we parted. "Now go. I'll call you when I have more information." He hailed a cab.

Once I was in the back seat, I observed the scene out the rear window. The driver was about to navigate into traffic. It was then I remembered.

"Stop!" I startled the cab driver.

"You wanna get out or what?" He snapped back.

"No, just wait a minute—" I touched the button and the window descended. "Jerard!" I flailed my arm. He was about to get into another cab.

"What is it, Sarah?"

"I remembered something else."

He muttered to the man behind the wheel and ran over to me.

I ducked my head out of the window. "The girl in the park, I think she had a box of candy—maybe chocolates—on her lap. Is that helpful?"

"You have no idea. Thanks." He turned away and sprinted back to his cab.

I took one last glance through the rear window and slumped into the cracked leather seat. Losing my job no longer overwhelmed me. At least I was alive and could get another position. The murdered women no longer had that choice.

28
CHAPTER

It had begun to rain again, and the rhythm of the cab's wipers calmed me. I wanted to go home, gather up my dogs, and sink into the couch. I checked my watch—nearly 3:00 p.m.

"Where to?" The cabby asked.

"Take me to 2120 Dolores Street, please."

"Gotcha." The cabby pulled into traffic as the rain pounded the windshield.

My eyebrows squeezed tight as I concentrated on solving the crumbling puzzle surrounding these girls' deaths. My cellphone rang inside my purse. I hesitated. Who was calling now? Someone else wanting to slam a few more bullets in me? I should have turned the damned thing off. My hand sifted through my purse and found my phone. Nicole's caller ID flashed. I could ignore it, but it might be nice to hear a familiar voice.

"Hi, Sarah. I have a big favor to ask." Her voice sounded hoarse.

"Your words are crackly. Are you okay?"

"I have the flu that's been going around. I wasn't feeling that great at lunch yesterday." She sneezed three times. "I have a gallery showing from five to seven, but I can't get out of bed. The caterer's supposed to be there at four to set up."

"Sorry you're not feeling well, but I have to tell you about what just happened with Jerard." I shifted in the seat but I could not get comfortable.

"Tell me later. My stomach's tumbling again. The gallery owner also has the flu. Would you be able to cover for me tonight?"

My head dropped against the seat back and I closed my eyes. I wanted the quietness of my own home. "Oh, Nicole, I've had the worst day. I was laid off from work this morning, and then I ran into Jerard. He dropped an overflowing box of information on me. He's not the person I thought he was. It's so overwhelming—I have no energy left to go into it right now. I also don't have it in me to be charming at an art sale. Why don't you try calling Liz?" I looked out the cab window: a thick layer of rolling fog displaced the rain.

Nicole wheezed into the phone. Since she hadn't drilled me on the Jerard incident, I figured she *must* be sick.

She continued. "I already asked Liz. She's working at a Children's Home fundraiser in Sausalito tonight. This showing is important. I have a buyer coming in from Malibu who plans on purchasing a table and two chairs—a four-thousand-dollar sale for me. What if I offer you a four-hundred-dollar commission?"

"Well, I'm without a job—I could use the money." I chewed on a fingernail.

"Everything is set up for the showing. The newspaper printed a small blurb, along with a picture of the owner and me in the Sunday arts section."

"Are you expecting a big turnout?" Maybe she could reschedule for another day. I held my breath, hoping for this possibility. "What about the owner?"

"No, remember, I told you she also has the flu. We've had quite a few RSVPs."

"Oh." I said in a monotone voice. I could not come up with any more reasons to get out of this obligation.

"The exhibit is at the Uno Gallery at Post and Taylor. You can grab the key and alarm code from the dress shop next door. We should have canceled, but we need the sales. Bill hired a guard. He was nervous about me being there without security after that girl was found in the park."

The day dropped me into the eye of a tornado that chucked me to the side of the road. The image of the girl in the park flickered in front of me. "Did you say that Bill hired a guard for your exhibit?" Maybe if Bill hadn't done this, I'd be able to excuse my way out of this event.

"Yes, the guard will be there tonight." Her tone was abrasive.

Was she becoming impatient with me? Well, she could just listen to my problems for a minute or two. "You need to hear what Jerard told me today."

"Sarah, later. I may not make it to the bathroom." She hacked into the phone.

Was I giving in again, like I always did? Here I was, letting another person run my life. On the other hand, I'd worked Nicole's exhibits before. The debate in my head told me who was winning—Nicole. "All right, I'll do it, but this is the last time I'm running interference for you. I'm going to have to go home and change. I won't be able to make it by four, so the caterer will have to wait."

"Thank you so much. I'm going to throw up now," Nicole croaked.

I watched the cab drive off, the sound of its engine muffled by fog. I fastened my coat collar tighter around my neck and headed up the stairs. An unshakeable sense of fear entered my mind. Was the killer still in the city?

I fed the dogs and let them run in the backyard for a few minutes. Then I changed into a pair of black pants and topped a red silk blouse with a black blazer. My hair was a frizzy mess from the rain, but I had time enough to run a brush through it and put on lipstick. I dropped the pups off at the Ackermanns' at 4:20 p.m., caught a cab, and headed to the gallery.

The fog thickened so the driver and I could barely see the car in front of us. Was the killer out there on the street waiting for his next victim? A chill captured me even though the heater inside the cab was blasting. People crowded the street corners, then headed home from work. If only I were one of them.

I asked the driver to let me out at the corner of Post where I spotted a newspaper machine. I wanted to see if there was any advertisement for tonight's art showing. I paid the cabbie and exited. Once at the metal box, I dropped in three quarters and removed the *Daily*.

The words SERIAL KILLER SUSPECTED IN SAN FRANCISCO MURDER screamed across the front page, and a photograph of the latest victim splashed under the headline.

Sandra Walker had lived in San Mateo and worked at the Bel Air Art Gallery in Millbrae. Photos of the previous victims were featured below hers. All the women had brown, shoulder-length hair and maybe were in their mid-thirties. Their eyes held my attention, especially those of Joe's sister, Clarissa. Her eyes were the same deep brown ovals as Nicole's. I could not imagine the pain Joe went through after his sister was murdered. I folded the paper and pressed it to my chest.

29
CHAPTER

The light changed green, and I crossed over to the Uno Gallery. The caterer leaned against the doorway; he smoked a cigarette and held a large, cylinder-shaped server. The lights in the window illuminated Nicole's beautiful mosaic table, along with two watercolor paintings by the gallery owner, Leslie Burns.

I spotted the caterer. "I'll be right there. I have to pick up the key next door." I ducked into Renee's Designs dress shop and retrieved the key and alarm code from the owner. All this rushing shortened my breath.

I came around to the gallery entrance and unlocked the door. A small bell hanging over the door rang as I entered. "Sorry I'm late," I said to the caterer, "but I think we can get everything set up by five o'clock." I held the door open for him. "I'm filling in for the owners, Leslie and Nicole. They both have the flu."

The caterer shrugged his shoulders as if he didn't care. He started to come in; a cigarette dangled from his mouth.

"Would you mind putting that out?" I pointed to the disgusting thing between his lips.

He jerked the cigarette from his mouth, went outside, and ground it under the heel of his shoe.

"Thank you."

"Yeah, whatever." He mumbled something under his breath.

I searched for the light switch and found it next to the door. I flicked it on. Nicole and Leslie's artworks were beautifully displayed, and special lighting over each piece brought them to life. The alarm system beeped next to the coat rack. I put in the four-number code and the noise ceased.

The caterer strode through the gallery toward a small kitchenette tucked in the back.

I followed and asked, "Have you worked the showings here before?" I was trying my best to be civil to this jerk. I could hear him opening and closing drawers and cupboards.

"Yeah. I've done about three jobs here. Where the hell are the serving utensils? Never mind—I found them."

I wasn't in the mood for this guy. Hopefully, he'd set up and shut up.

I turned as I heard the bell jingle, and a scrawny guy, about five-foot-seven, entered. "I'm Jeff," he said, "the security guard for tonight." Both hands were on his hips, feet apart, and he was obviously trying to act the part of a tough guy.

The guy couldn't weigh more than one hundred and fifty pounds. I sure hoped he had a black belt in karate.

"I'm Sarah." I shook his hand.

His weak handshake knocked down my confidence. He said, "I'll just stand outside the door if that's okay?"

I started to say "fine," but he didn't wait for an answer and went outside. Well, I was surrounded by an ass of a caterer and a guard who might need my help taking down a bad guy. My mind jumped to the killer. Here I was at a gallery. What was I thinking, taking on this showing? *Stop. Just get through the night.*

I popped into the kitchenette. "Do you need any help?"

"Nah, I got it." The caterer opened the cylinder server and unloaded what appeared to be a chocolate-chip cheesecake. I watched him retrieve a large knife from a drawer, and—with perfect strokes—he sliced the cake into small sections which he placed on a silver tray. He filled a crystal-cut bowl with fresh strawberries. Champagne glasses lined another tray. He may have been an ass, but he appeared to know what he was doing.

I left him to his work and proceeded to the corner desk in the main gallery. I took off my coat, draped it over the chair, and tossed the newspaper on top of the desk. I slid open one of the drawers and tucked my purse inside. I checked the small room off the main gallery, flicked on the lights, and saw Nicole's table and chair set that she hoped to sell tonight. I wandered over to another exit door in the far corner of the room and made sure it was locked. I did not want more than one entrance to the showing.

I returned to the main gallery. The caterer set the table in the center of the room. He draped it with a burgundy tablecloth and arranged a stack of china dessert plates and silver forks. Small paper napkins with Uno Gallery imprinted in gold fanned out in front of the plates. Champagne sparkled in the glass flutes.

My stomach made a few growling sounds—all I'd eaten today was a half-wilted salad. I thought of having a slice of cheesecake, but I needed protein, not a sugar high and drop, to get through tonight.

The caterer emerged from the kitchenette. "Okay, I'm taking off." With his server in hand, he stalked out the front door.

Wow, the guy really needs a few lessons in social skills. I retrieved my phone from my blazer pocket and checked the time—5:20 p.m. I clicked off my cellphone and settled it on the desk next to a small CD player. I sifted through the stack of CDs and chose some smooth jazz. Soon the music helped soften my insides.

The jingle of the bell announced the first two guests—a man and woman, both wearing raincoats. Time to turn on the charm.

"Welcome. Here, let me hang up your coats." I placed their wraps on the rack by the door. The woman sported a diamond ring. He wore a perfectly tailored suit. Maybe they had money to spend; it might be a good night for sales.

The main gallery filled with a respectable-sized crowd. Fifteen or so people. One couple stood for at least ten minutes in front of Leslie's watercolor of two girls wading in the ocean. A young woman appeared from the smaller gallery carrying a mosaic vase.

I approached her. "May I help you?"

"I have the perfect place at home for this vase." She cradled it closely. "I also love the table and chair set the artist made, but it's out of my price range." Her shoulders deflated a bit.

She followed me to the desk. I folded bubbled wrap around the mosaic and nested it in a box of foam peanuts. The lid was embossed with the same gold letters as the napkins. I completed the sale and delivered her a receipt. "I'm so glad you're taking home one of Nicole's pieces. She's a wonderful artist."

She embraced the box and I watched her exit the gallery. The cheesecake was dwindling down to a few slices. I ambled around and topped off customers' champagne glasses. My wristwatch spelled out 6:30 p.m. Where was that buyer from Malibu?

Someone touched my shoulder. "Excuse me." It was the couple that had been admiring Leslie's seaside scene. "We'd like to buy that painting." They pointed across the room.

"Of course. I saw you admiring it earlier." I eased the painting off the easel and carried it to the desk. I yanked a long swath of brown paper from a roll mounted on the wall and made my wrapping job resemble that of a professional. Duct tape was the only thing I could find, so I cut it in strips and secured the paper around the frame. I wrote up the sale and presented the couple their painting.

"Enjoy," I said. Two sales. Now, if this Bruce guy would show up to buy Nicole's table and chairs, it would be quite a successful night.

When I heard the bell tinkle, I stood behind the desk, adding the receipt to the cash box. A tall, gorgeous man caused that irritating bell to ring again. I was sure his sandy-colored hair and facial bone structure lured women. He was dressed in a pale-blue sweater and tan slacks; he wore a pair of expensive Italian loafers. A model straight out of a Southern California magazine.

He must be Malibu Bruce. Definitely not dressed for San Francisco. He hung his umbrella on the coat rack. He ran his hands through his hair as he traveled around the room before stopping in front of one of Nicole's mosaic lamps.

I came out from behind the desk and glided toward him. "May I help you?"

He smoothed a hand over Nicole's lamp. "Oh, hello." I must have startled him because he almost knocked over the object. "Jeez — sorry. I guess if I break it, I buy it."

Too tired for a clever comeback, I introduced myself. "By any chance are you Bruce Harper?"

He nodded. "I saw Nicole's work in an art magazine and knew I had to have some of her pieces. Of course, her photograph also had something to do with my wanting to meet her." His fingers caressed the lamp.

Was his real plan to ask Nicole out? I guessed he did not know she was married. Was he here to buy her art or hit on her? There went my mind again. *Concentrate, Sarah.*

"Is Nicole here? I can't wait to meet her." He clasped his hands together.

"She has the flu."

He squeezed his lips and his shoulders slumped.

"She knew you were coming tonight possibly to buy the mosaic table and chairs. Come this way."

He followed me to the smaller gallery where he spotted the table and chairs in the corner. The joy that spread across his face said, "Sold!" I was going to have an extra four hundred dollars in my checking account.

"It's beautiful." He meandered around the table and between the two chairs. "The colors are so much brighter than the magazine photo. I know a fantastic photographer in Malibu who would capture her work on a strong professional level." He sat down in one of the chairs. "Perfect fit."

What was with this guy? He wanted to set up Nicole with his photographer, and then he acted as if he was in a romantic interlude with a chair? He was getting a little creepy.

187

He slapped his hands together. "Yes, I'm taking all three pieces."

Creepy or not, I went to get the receipt book. The gallery emptied its customers, except for Malibu Bruce. I went behind the desk and checked my watch—7:20 p.m. I called back to Bruce. "Did you want to pay by check or credit card?"

"Credit." He toured the main gallery. While I wrote up the transaction and his shipping information, he slipped over to the dessert table, picked up a flute of champagne, and took a few sips.

"Nicole's going to be so happy. I'll let her know how much you appreciate her work." I put the final receipt in the cash box and handed Bruce his copy. I was hoping he'd finish his champagne and leave. I wanted to get home and go to bed.

The security guard poked his head in the door. "You mind if I take off now? I was only hired 'til seven o'clock, and it's almost seven-thirty now." His hand tapped the doorjamb.

"You can leave." I signaled with a raised palm.

I didn't want to be alone while closing the gallery. "Bruce, would you mind staying while I lock up and get a cab?"

"Sure, no problem." He sipped the rest of his champagne.

I retrieved my coat off the chair. "We had a murder here in the city and I'm a bit on edge."

"I read about it. Police seem to think it's linked to one that happened in Southern California some months ago." He set down his glass and came over to the desk. "Hey, I don't know about you, but I'm starving. I don't really know where to go for dinner. Why don't you join me? We could share a cab."

I jerked at the drawer and withdrew my purse. Over my shoulder, I said, "I've had a long day and I just want to go home."

I heard him exhale. "Do you mind if I take one more glimpse of my purchase before I go?" He raised his eyebrows.

Bruce had spent four grand. It was the least I could do.

"Sure, go ahead." I was about to plop down in a chair when that damned bell jingled again. I should have locked the door.

30
CHAPTER

Tom. What a surprise. "Hey, what are you doing here? I'm getting ready to close up." Even though I was exhausted, his face comforted me.

"Sorry I'm late — got stuck behind a car accident." He sailed across the room and planted a peck on my cheek. "Wanted to come by and see Nicole's exhibit." He ducked his head into the kitchen. "Where is she?"

Why didn't he just turn around and go home? That's where I wanted to be. I squeezed my thighs.

He came back to the desk and set his briefcase on the floor.

I threw my hands in the air. "Nicole and the owner have the flu. So here I am — Miss Dependable."

"I'd planned on purchasing a few pieces for my restaurant. Can I take a quick tour? I have my car; I could drive you home." He shoved his hands in his pockets and rocked back on his heels.

"Listen, Tom, I'll let her know you came by. The exhibit will be up for two weeks, so you can come back when she's better. Right now, I just want to lock up and get out of here." I took the keys out of my purse and rattled them.

"Okay, but I insist on driving you home. I don't want you out there by yourself with this serial killer."

The keys fell to the floor. Why did he have to bring that up? I bent to pick them up—my hand shook. Maybe it was from hunger. Or had his comment about the murdered women put me on edge?

Tom rubbed his hand across his lips. "You have any water?"

"Might be some bottled water in the refrigerator." I pointed toward the kitchen. He had done so much for me.

Tom vanished into the kitchen.

Dishes and glasses remained on the refreshment table. I tossed keys, purse, and coat on a chair, retrieved a stack of plates, and dragged my tired body to the kitchen.

"Hey, Tom, maybe you can help me clean up before I leave."

"No problem." He took a swig of bottled water. I lowered the dishes in the sink and then trailed him back into the gallery. As he passed the desk he paused and peered down at the newspaper.

"Those poor girls. Is this the one you saw in the park?" His finger touched her photo.

I peered over his shoulder. "Yes. I'm glad you were there with me." I lowered my head on his shoulder and shut my eyes. If only I could erase those images, especially Clarissa's.

"You know," he said, "they're all similar, aren't they?" He inspected the front page. "This third one reminds me of Nicole."

"So I've heard. That's why Nicole's husband hired a security guard." I pointed to the front door. "He didn't want her here alone." I massaged my neck. A headache crept in—I hoped it wasn't going to turn into a migraine. "Let's finish cleaning up and get out of here."

We retrieved the last of the dishes and headed back to the kitchen.

Tom filled the sink with soap and hot water. He started washing a plate, but then he hesitated. "Hey, how's it going with that guy at the restaurant? What's his name?"

"Jerard. We've been seeing each other. I found out some things today about him that really surprised me."

"Sarah?" A voice called from the gallery. *Bruce.* I forgot he was here.

"Who's that?" Tom said, as he finished rinsing the last of the dishes.

"He bought Nicole's mosaic table and chairs." I threw him a towel.

"Nice." He took over drying.

I hurried to the front gallery where Bruce stood by

the desk, seeming absorbed in the newspaper. I said, "I have a ride home now. Thanks for staying with me."

"Okay. Please let Nicole know that I'll contact her about a photo shoot of her work. I'm thinking of staying in town for a few more days. Maybe she'll be over the flu by then and we can meet." He shook my hand.

"Thanks. I'll let her know." Should I tell her? He seemed more interested in Nicole than her art. I watched Bruce retrieve his umbrella and evaporate into the night. I went back to the kitchen, about to tell Tom about my day, when that annoying bell rang yet again. Why hadn't I locked the door? I came around the corner of the kitchen—Joe was planted in the center of the gallery. What was going on? Next thing I knew, Jerard would show up.

Going home was the only thing on my mind. I didn't feel like having a long conversation with Joe. He behaved differently. Was he nervous? He tugged on his tie.

"Jerard wanted me to come by and give you a ride home. It took him a while to find out where you were. Your cell phone kept going to voicemail."

"I turned it off for the showing and forgot to turn it back on. I have a ride home and I'm closing up now. Please thank him for me."

"He told me not to take no for an answer, and he explained why in great detail. It has to do with the serial killer. He'd have come himself, but he and Paul are heading over to Daly City with a search warrant for the suspect's home."

"Everything okay out here?" Tom emerged from the kitchen while wiping off a knife with a dish towel.

I turned to Tom. "They think they've found the killer. He lives in Daly City like you. Jerard sent Joe to pick me up."

When I faced Joe, he took a large stride forward and gripped my arm so tightly I moaned.

"Let go! What are you doing?" My voice was shrill.

"Please, Sarah, just let Jerard explain a few things." His eyes were not on me, but on Tom.

In an instant Tom sprang to Joe's side.

31
CHAPTER

Joe's fingers dug into my shoulders. He rose on the balls of his feet and his mouth opened; then his legs folded and he dropped to the floor. I sucked in a painful breath, bent down, and touched his face.

"It's Tom," he whispered through labored breath. "He killed my sister." His eyes fluttered open. I tucked one hand under his neck and the other around his shoulder, trying to hoist him up. Something was wet. I drew my hand away—blood was smeared across my palm.

I peered up and saw the knife in Tom's hand. Streaks of red covered a section of the silver blade. Joe's blood. Tom backed away toward the entrance. He locked the door, then seized the edge of the front window curtains and slid them across, shutting us off from the outside world.

I shouted, "Help!" But then I remembered—I let the guard go home. My stomach twisted into knots.

Tom picked the dish towel off the floor and wiped the blood from the knife.

I kept my hold on Joe. "Tom, what have you done — and why?" The words stuck in my mouth.

He raced over and bent down, jerking my arm upward with such force that my feet left the floor.

The next sound came from Joe, his voice shallow and forced. "Sarah, run —." Then his words stopped as if someone had turned off a faucet.

"*You* murdered those girls?" Who was this man? I thought I knew him.

His face flushed with anger, but ice replaced the soft blue of his eyes. "It wasn't supposed to end this way. I had so many plans for us now that your career's taking off. Sadly, things will have to change." He pointed to Joe. "Open his jacket and get his cell phone."

I hesitated.

"Now!" He angled the knife tip toward me.

I rummaged through Joe's jacket and found his phone. Tom extracted it from my grip and crushed it under his heel. He yanked me up so hard, I thought my shoulder had dislocated.

I screamed and he intensified the knife pressure against my neck. "Shut up or I'll slice open your beautiful porcelain throat." With the point of the knife, he lifted a strand of hair off my face and slid the blade down the side of my neck.

"Okay." My thoughts fumbled around. If only I could think of some way to escape. When I tried to snag my phone off the counter, Tom wrenched me backward.

He tossed my phone on the floor and smashed it to pieces. He laid the knife on the newspaper. Blood drops smudged the photos of the murdered girls. The similarities were strong. A thought gut punched me. Tom was here for Nicole.

Not long afterward, the gallery phone rang, jarring Tom enough for me to slip out of his hold and make a run for the front door. Tom grabbed the back of my blazer—I heard the sound of ripping cloth. He hauled me against his chest and wrapped his arm around my neck. I managed to scratch his arm, and warm liquid oozed onto my fingertips.

"Stop struggling." His spittle struck the side of my face. I'd never heard his voice filled with such rage.

He said, "I don't mind a little fight, it adds to the thrill." Hands tightened around my throat, and my breathing became shallow, strained. My feet floated off the floor; my body slumped forward. I saw pitch black—after that, nothing.

When I woke up, my dogs were scampering around my ankles. I couldn't move my hands or feet, and I was hunched over. *Oh no.* What I had thought were dachsunds at my feet were two gray rats, their long tails slithering around my legs. Why couldn't I move my hands? They were tied to the sides of a wooden chair, and my feet were bound to its legs. I could hear bus horns honking outside.

I cried out but the tape across my mouth muffled the sound. My throat pain made it difficult to swallow. My brain did a rewind—I pictured Tom squeezing my neck. I blinked; my eyes adjusted to the light. I raised off the floor, hoping the noise of the chair legs hitting concrete would alert someone. One of the rats scratched the top of my foot. I let out a distorted yelp, which made them dart away in different directions.

A strong odor of mold invaded my nostrils. I shivered in the cold and dampness penetrated my pores. Somewhere a light switched on. Footsteps lumbered down the stairs on the other side of the wall. Was someone going to save me?

Was music playing? Maybe from the opera *La Bohème*? From my skewed position, I managed to examine all sides of the room. I must have been in the basement of the gallery.

Tom veered around the corner with a grin that made me sick to my stomach. He crept toward me, apparently savoring the moment. One hand held his briefcase, the other, the gallery's CD player which discharged loud and grating arias. He deposited both items on a shelf.

He stood for a few seconds studying me before he hovered over my chair, bent down, and ground his fingertips into my thighs. His palms inched up my legs. Was he hoping to get a response? The duct tape over my mouth held back the scream. I would not give him the pleasure of hearing it.

"You're awake, welcome back. I brought the player down so we could enjoy a little music. I know how you love opera. Remember our college days, waiting for half-price theater tickets?" Tom's familiar voice, the one I'd heard for years, the soft, confident tone that encouraged my singing career but no longer existed. Instead, these words stole away my sanity where I sat tied to the chair.

He shoved his hands off my thighs, causing a sharp pinching pain. His left hand ran through my hair, lifting strands in the air, then letting them drift down. He circled behind me and mumbled in my ear.

He said, "I'm not happy about what I'm about to do. I normally enjoy the kill, but with you it's different. I have no choice. I can't get you into a cab without you screaming. So, I'll have to take care of you here. Guess it's time for me to find a new place to live. Police won't find me. I'm invisible."

When the heat of his breath hit my ear, my stomach clenched. I thumped up and down, and the chair made loud, banging noises as its legs hit the concrete. A cracking sound came from the aged wood.

"Relax, Sarah. I'd tell you something encouraging like 'I won't hurt you,' but you probably know by now that would be a lie." He paced around and halted in front of me; his smirk suggested he was amused.

What now? Would I be on the front-page tomorrow?

He slithered over to a corner of the room, picked up a chair, and dropped it in front of mine. His face was so close I could smell his perspiration. His dark eyes shone like slivers of black ice.

He locked my chin in one hand, progressively tightening his grip. "I'm not used to performing murders in the basement of a gallery. I prefer the comfort of a storage unit. It takes planning and research to find a rental space near my murders, but I've managed. It's all about the timing. I don't want rigor mortis to set in before I place my girls at their final destinations. I have to dress them and comb their hair." He shoved my face hard before releasing his hand. "Joe's screwed up all my plans. I love you, Sarah; I have since college."

God, Tom, you're really thinking of killing me.

He slouched back and crossed his arms and legs. "I like the feel of the outdoors. I always arrange my girls next to a tree overlooking a lake. Remember the girl you saw in the park? I watched as one of your little rat dogs ran over to her, sniffing. You got to witness my work up close. Your terrified face that day is embedded in my mind forever."

I remembered him holding me, making me feel safe. All a lie.

A low laugh rumbled from his chest; my skin crawled. "You know, I was disappointed that I couldn't take in her scent one last time. I wanted to share that moment with you, and I tried not to laugh when you grabbed your mutt and ran toward me. I brought you into my arms, consoling you, rubbing your back. Your face was the color of fog."

If only I could reason with his twisted monologue.

He let his head drop. "I hadn't planned on that last kill, but when you asked me to meet you in the park Wednesday, I couldn't resist. I wanted to show off for you. When I read about Nicole's event in the paper, I couldn't pass up the opportunity to be in the same gallery. I wasn't sure I was going to kill her, so I decided to make that decision when I got here. I'm disappointed my long-time experiment with you is going to end. Remember how insecure you were in college? I had to encourage you to sing."

Distract him, agree with him. I pretended I was interested.

"I've put in a lot of hours on you and we were almost there. I've got a huge contract ready for you to sign. Of course, Jerard had your attention for the last week or so. You'll get a kick out of hearing this—I spied on you and Jerard the day you followed him into the galleries. Been keeping close tabs on him. After doing a little investigating, I figured he was asking a lot of questions about the murdered women. I think he might be an undercover cop or detective."

"Tom, stop this." My words came out a muffled mess.

"What's that? Are you trying to say something I could care less about?" His fingers played with the edge of the tape and then he ripped it off.

My eyes watered—the skin around my mouth was on fire. Words exploded from my mouth like firecrackers. "He was a police officer and now he's a private investigator. You bastard. You killed those women!"

32
CHAPTER

He uncrossed his legs, stood up, and stretched—as if this was another ordinary day. He paced back and forth at a methodically timed pace. "The police are piecing things together. The FBI's onto my killing spree. The problem's Jerard. Nicole *had* to do her little matchmaker number. That's one more reason why I wanted to tie one of my red scarves around her neck and choke her blue. Bitch!" His face reddened; he traipsed over to the brief-case, then released the latches. He dragged out a box with a piece of red material hanging from its edge and removed something, but I couldn't see what it was.

"Tom, you need help." I gave my wrists a violent twist, trying to loosen the cord around them.

He returned to his chair and faced me. In one hand he held a box of chocolate-covered cherries adorned with a purple satin ribbon. A red sheer scarf dangled off the index finger of his other hand. My gut double knotted.

"Enough with the 'I need help crap.' I've heard it before. I'm going to explain to you what's about to happen. I like sharing this process with my soon-to-be trophies. But you're not one of my usual girls."

My eyes focused on the two items.

He set the candy box on the floor and tied the scarf around my neck. A sharp tug completed his knot. "You'll be different. I'll miss you. I had so many plans for us—I thought eventually we'd make a perfect couple."

The calmer I stayed, the better.

He picked up the box and unsealed the lid. The scent of cocoa drifted through the air. He held up one piece. "Chocolate?"

When he held it in front of my mouth, I jerked my head away. I inhaled, but the shaft of air—a sharp sliver of ice—pierced my lungs. The music continued playing loudly in the background, though the fear in my mind was even louder. He popped the chocolate in his mouth, tossed the box to the floor, and then disappeared behind my chair.

The trembling inside me turned into a full-blown earthquake. "Don't do this." I scanned the wall hiding the stairwell and fought to stay in control.

"Funny. They all want to figure me out. I tell them the story of my dear mother, the artist who took off on me. And my dad—a controlling prick. I understood why she wanted to get away from him, but she could have taken me with her."

206

"Is this all about your mother?" I shouted above the music.

He hoisted my chair off the floor. His strength was over the top. My feet dangled in the air.

"Shut up and let me finish." Tom slammed the chair down on the concrete with a loud thud. A sharp pain shot up my spine causing me a severe migraine.

He came back into view, sat down in his chair, and combed both hands through his hair. Was he deciding to send me to an early grave?

"Okay, let's play psychiatrist and patient. I was twelve. She left. Dad thought she'd come back. He preserved her studio like a shrine. She never came back. Six years later Dad had a massive heart attack surrounded by her paintings. I found him spread out on the floor, clutching one of her brushes. Now, isn't that one of the saddest stories?"

"Dammit! What the hell happened? You were mad at your mother, so you decided to kill women? Did they resemble her? The killing didn't bring her back, did it?" The cords chafed my hands.

"Quiet, or I'll put the tape back on."

There had to be something I could do to stop him. I rocked the chair from side to side. "Are you going to murder me the same way you killed the others?" Then I butted him with my head.

He rubbed his forehead. "Well, damn, Sarah, finally

you're showing some spirit. You need to calm down."

"I won't, you asshole." I spat the words in his face.

When Tom reapplied the tape, I bit down on his fingers. He belted me—my chair tumbled on its side and my head slammed into the concrete. Had someone crashed a frying pan against my skull? I didn't want to die. I had so much to look forward to—singing, marriage, maybe children.

Tom returned my chair to an upright position. The room spun; something ripped. More duct tape. He secured it across my mouth—his coarse thumbs constricted my breathing. If I had never seen evil before, I witnessed it in his contorted face.

The room closed in. Was I losing consciousness again?

33
CHAPTER

The pain on the side of my head reminded me of my whereabouts. I moved my wrists, but they were still bound and rubbed raw from my tugging at the cords. *Concentrate—get your strength back. Maybe Tom's changed his mind.* I thought about Max and Gracey. Who would take care of them if something happened to me? The Ackermanns? Tears burned my eyes and tumbled down my cheeks.

That depressing opera music blared from the CD player. I surveyed what was in front of me. Where did he go?

Someone whacked my chair from behind, and my teeth bit my tongue. I tasted blood.

He mumbled in my ear. "I always do a trial run before the final destination. It's as if my girls are suspended between life and death. You're a fighter, Sarah, and growing stronger. Too bad it's too late. How's your head, by the way?"

His fingers yanked a strand of my hair. I jerked my head to the side. The pain increased with every attack.

"I'll take the tape off if you promise to keep your voice down. We wouldn't want anyone to hear us, would we?" He snickered and took his time peeling off the tape, drawing out my agony.

"Oh my," he smirked, "the side of your head is starting to bruise and swell." He drove his fingers into the wound, knowing it would send me further misery. "The mortician will have some fun covering that up." Tom hovered like a bird about to dive for its prey.

You sadistic bastard.

He approached me again, but this time he held a knife, the same one he'd used to stab Joe. How could I forget about Joe? Was he alive?

Tom returned to his chair and placed the knife on the floor. His hands came toward me; his calloused thumbs dug into the middle of my throat. I coughed—his eyes widened. I used what little energy I had to jerk away. I screamed, gasped for air, and shifted sideways. *Girl, this is no time to be the quiet one in the room. Don't give up—fight!*

"Shut up, bitch!" His hands flew off my neck. He bent down, picked up the knife, and pointed it at me. His perfectly styled hair fell out of place: blond strands swept across his eyes. Dark circles of sweat formed under his arms.

I inhaled while I could. "You think I'm going to sit here tied to this crappy wooden chair and let you kill me?" I hurled the words in his face. "Boo hoo, your mother deserted you. Well, let me tell you, life sucks sometimes. You could stop now and let me go. You'll stand trial, go to jail, and face a possible death sentence. Or you could make me another notch on your belt, but believe me, you won't take me without a fight." I thrust the chair up and down, listening to the wood crack.

"Nice speech. Most of my girls just cry and beg. I've never seen this side of you. You usually just give in and give up. I knew you were changing when you got up on that stage."

Tom backed toward the staircase wall. Something shining halfway up the edge of the barrier caught my eye. Light came from a small window. Headlights of a passing car? What was it? A mirror? There it was again—a small mirror!

Tom must have witnessed my glance darting away. He relocated behind me, drew my chair close, and yanked the top of my head while clutching my hair to his chest. As he dragged me farther away from the walled staircase, my chair tilted backward.

A shadow came around the corner of the wall. A gun pointed in our direction. Tom pressed the cold tip of the knife against my neck. The opera played its final note and the CD clicked off. A stream of adrenalin, fear, and hope flooded my veins.

Within seconds Tom's voice rose to a higher pitch. "Son of a bitch—Jerard—what the hell are you doing here?"

My mind registered—was that Jerard standing in front of me? I nudged my head, trying to distance my throat from the knife, but Tom regained his grip. He edged the tip of the knife lightly across my throat, and a sharp sting penetrated my skin.

"Huh!" escaped from my mouth.

"Tom, stop! It's over," Jerard demanded.

Something wet was dripping down my neck. I couldn't tell, but it must have been my blood. The cut must not have been deep because I was breathing. *Don't pass out now.*

Seconds went by. Jerard gripped the gun as he aimed it at Tom. "Drop the knife on the floor. Listen to me, Sarah. You're going to be okay." His tone was even and confident.

I blinked a couple of times at the sound of my name. He was real—I wasn't imagining him. I let out a shaky "okay." After all I'd been through, how could Jerard say I was going to be all right? With the knife at my neck ready for its final performance, I couldn't afford to make a move.

Tom said, "It's not over. Let's have some more fun. You think I'm going to give up so quickly?" My back stiffened. "Hey, Sarah, do you have any words you'd like to share with your boyfriend before we end this?"

"Just give up. You can't get out of this. It's over." The words fell out of my mouth—I doubted they'd do any good.

"The only way you're leaving this room, Tom, is if you give up." Jerard jerked the gun and took another step forward. His slow approach put him about five feet away.

"Curious. How'd you know it was me?" Tom eased his grip on my hair.

"It took a lot of time, but Paul and I finally put all the pieces together. I was a lieutenant for the Tampa Police Department, and now I'm a private investigator."

"Umm. I didn't get a good feeling from you the first night I met you at my restaurant." Tom spilled the words into my ear. "I also didn't like all the time you spent with my protégée."

Jerard said, "You murdered my brother's fiancée, Clarissa Kazakian. Remember her?"

"Of course. Cute little thing. Considered letting her live, but I just couldn't help myself."

Jerard's eyes leveled at Tom. How could he remain so calm? I was holding onto one ounce of strength. I finally found someone I can trust, and I might die. If I survived—not if—but when—Tom was locked up, I was going to give my relationship with Jerard a solid try.

Jerard continued his story. "I wasn't getting any-where by staying on at the police department. My brother and I decided to do some investigating on our own. I got my private investigator's license and my brother set me up on salary. Joe, the man you stabbed upstairs is Clarissa's brother. For your information, he's alive."

213

"Guess I should have gone a little deeper with this knife." Tom snorted.

Jerard wouldn't let Tom distract him. "You don't alter your habits, Tom. Some specifics, like the box of chocolate-covered cherries, were never given to reporters.

"Did you appreciate that small gesture? I liked leaving candy for my girls. Mother loved it." The hand holding the knife relaxed.

Jerard broke in. "The murders traveled along the coastline—Savannah, Tampa, Galveston. So after Los Angeles, the next logical place would be San Francisco."

"I probably should have skipped the murder here, but I couldn't resist. It was time for me to share my passion with Sarah. She knows I'm a stickler for detail, don't you?" After jerking my head back, Tom glared at me.

Jerard's voice forced Tom's attention back to him, and he said, "I started checking out art galleries along the way—San Luis Obispo, Half Moon Bay. I looked for owners or curators who matched the descriptions of the murdered girls. Shortly after I started visiting galleries in San Francisco, I met Nicole."

Tom let go of my head and I shivered at the sound of her name. *Nicole.* My insides thrashed.

"Sarah, focus on me." Jerard's words brought me back. He went on, "I started researching all the men who were close to Nicole, including you. By the way, I discovered you'd traveled a lot."

Tom shrugged. "I like to try restaurants in different cities. No harm in that."

"We found the murder dates matched your airline and train tickets. By using your real name, you made it fairly easy for us."

"Guess I screwed up a bit. I'll make sure I set up different travel plans next time. And there *will* be a next time."

Jerard edged slightly to his right.

I see what you're doing Jerard. Keep it up.

The knife slipped. Tom pressed his thumb against the lower part of my neck.

Jerard said, "The results from the DNA sample sent to the lab a month ago came back. I met with Paul at the police station. Your background check proved interesting. Arrested once for assault and battery on a woman when you were twenty-two.

"They swabbed your mouth and—*bingo*—you entered the database. Your DNA matched that found Karen Johnson's clothing. Remember her, the girl that got away?"

"Yeah, I remember that bitch. I clubbed her hard against the side of the head. Didn't hit her with enough force." Tom wrenched my hair—I swore he ripped strands out of my scalp.

"She was found along a road near the art gallery where she worked. Barely alive—in a coma for eight months. When she became conscious, she remembered what happened."

"I should have killed her when I had a chance. Sloppy job," Tom muttered.

Jerard took another small step in our direction. "You've been in and out of trouble since you were a young teen. Mother took off, controlling father. Guess what? Your mother didn't run away."

The knife drifted down and rested on my breast. If he cut me one more time, I'd bite his fingers off and stuff them down his damned throat.

"What kind of crap are you giving me? Mother left me and my dad." Tom's voice—a shrill, piercing pitch. "You don't know—you . . . don't know what you're . . . what you're . . . I don't." As he stuttered, his voice cracked.

"No? Paul and I were able to find out where your family lived. The police searched the house that you still own in Bar Harbor, Maine late this afternoon. Their K-9 dogs dug up some interesting bones in the backyard. We're not sure yet, but most likely they belong to your mother. They found a silver locket with an inscription inside. 'To Mother. Love, your son, Tom.' She never left—she was murdered, maybe by your father, and buried behind the garage."

The increasing compression of the knife on my breast made my chest contract.

Jerard took another step to the left.

Tom must have seen his movement. "Make another move, and I'll slice her." The pressure of the knife increased—something dropped on my lap. Must have been a button he cut from my blouse.

The hell if you'll slice me! I drove my body backward, knocking Tom off kilter. The knife propelled through the air and clinked onto the cement floor. I shoved to my right, tipped the chair over, and this time I heard wood shattering. My efforts finally paid off. Splinters hung off my hands and legs, but I was free.

Tom lost his balance and fell backward. "Shit!" He recovered and lunged. "If I'm going to die, you're coming with me, Sarah."

Jerard aimed his revolver and fired.

34
CHAPTER

In an instant Tom stormed by me and crashed into Jerard. Blood dripped down the back of his arm and soaked his starched white shirt. He seemed oblivious to having been shot. The gun flew out of Jerard's hand.

With one swift kick I managed to boot the knife in Jerard's direction. At last I had mobility. I pushed off the floor and, without a second thought, I hauled myself toward Jerard and Tom. Jerard delivered a powerful punch to the side of Tom's face; he moved in the direction of the knife, but not fast enough. Tom must have anticipated this move—he dove for the weapon. He rolled over and leaped up. Knife in hand, he lunged at Jerard. The blade vanished into Jerard's side. Blood splashed onto his coat. Tom readied to strike again.

"Tom!" My voice sounded unnatural as if someone else was speaking.

He turned to me and wielded the knife over his head, "I'm in control again. I always come back." His eyes bulged and his face contorted. He raved as I edged over to the gun lying about two feet away. Tom paced, avoiding my gaze. He continued his self-talk.

I bent down and wrapped my hands around the weapon. "Tom." Had I said his name? I wasn't sure. He stopped pacing and came face-to-face with the barrel of my gun. He'd plunge the knife into me if I didn't act. My finger pulled the cold metal trigger—something was crackling—like fireworks.

His body suspended—blood poured from his belly. He raised his face to mine. He looked disoriented; his mouth gaped, but no words came out. I descended into the eyes of someone I'd known and trusted. Glassy-eyed, he took a tentative step toward me. The knife dropped from his hand; the metal clanked on the cement. My hands shook but I kept the gun pointed at him. *Please don't make me shoot you again.*

Before he could reach me, his body aimed downward, a spiral in slow-motion. *Tom, you were my friend for years.* I lowered the gun; the first sting of tears hit my cheek.

He lay a crumpled mound on the floor. The eyes of a dead man transfixed me.

Blood oozed from Tom onto the floor; a red pool formed around him. My arms weighed a hundred pounds. Someone nudged my back—I flinched.

Jerard's emerald eyes came into view. "He's dead, Sarah. He can't hurt you or any more girls." After withdrawing the gun from my hand, he tucked it into his waistband. He removed some of the cords that dangled around my wrists and legs.

But then he clasped his side and moaned. He unfastened his coat. Blood dripped down his white shirt, and he applied pressure against the wound.

"You're hurt." I tried to lift his hand away from the injury, but it remained there. His other arm wrapped around me and drew me to his chest. His embrace brought a rush of warmth. We both survived and now had a chance to be together. I wanted that with this man more than anything.

Footsteps rattled down the staircase and startled me. My hold on Jerard increased. Another person came around the stairway wall. Who was it? I eased away from Jerard. I needed to focus — my vision was so blurry from banging my head.

Paul approached, his raincoat dripping water on the floor. His gun was drawn and pointed at Tom whose body was a heap in the middle of the room.

"Paul?" I said. "How did you and Jerard know where to find me?"

He strode over. "You're safe now. Joe kept close tabs on Nicole. She didn't leave the house to go to her showing. I called Bill and he filled me in on Nicole's illness and you taking over for her at the exhibit. We told Joe to head over here. Jerard and I spent the entire afternoon gathering evidence at the precinct. We were both headed to Tom's house when my gut told me Jerard needed to go to the gallery instead."

"I wanted to be there when you arrested Tom, but if you hadn't convinced me to check on Sarah . . ." Jerard shook his head. "I don't even want to think about what could have happened."

"I had two patrol officers drive him over here and I'm glad I did. Jerard called me when he found Joe." Paul stepped over to Tom, bent down, and probed his neck.

"Does he have a pulse?" Jerard asked.

He shook his head. "Dead."

"Oh—no." My hands trembled as I relived holding the gun and pulling the trigger.

"It's okay, Sarah." Jerard's hand caressed my face. "Slow, deep breaths." Jerard's voice was low and soft. He breathed in and out, teaching me this basic function.

Paul replaced his gun into the holster inside his jacket and returned to us. "I'm glad we got here when we did. Liz would have shot *me* between the eyes if I hadn't."

I nodded. "Thank you, both of you.

Paul focused on the blood trickling onto Jerard's shirt. "Man, are you shot?" He guided us to the stairs to sit down.

Jerard said, "No. Tom stabbed me." He pointed to the knife on the floor. "I'll be okay. I want to help wrap this up. I've worked too hard to miss seeing this to the end."

Paul hollered up the stairwell. "Get another ambulance here—now!"

"Yes, sir." A voice from above answered.

"God, I shot him." I sobbed.

"And you saved our lives." Jerard's voice lowered in reverence.

I took deep breaths. My body was dropping to the temperature of a freezer locker. The room was shrinking. I wanted to cry, but my tears were locked up tight. *Come on, girl. You got through all this. Keep going.*

Jerard attempted to untie the red scarf from my neck with one hand as the other clutched his injured side. Paul extracted a plastic evidence bag from his pocket and I dropped the scarf briefcase, and CD player. Would I ever be able to listen to *La Bohème* again? *Damn you, Tom.* Why didn't I see who he truly was?

Anger replaced the fear in my veins. "To tell you the truth, Jerard, even if you hadn't shown up, I wasn't about to let this piece of shit kill me. Not sure how, but it wasn't going to happen." *My insides were telling me it was true—I'd made a breakthrough. Even though my body was suffering from exhaustion, a strength had grown inside me, and that new power was taking up permanent residence.* "Wait, what about Joe? We need to find out if he's okay." I struggled to rise in order to head up the stairs.

Jerard took my arm and sat me back down. "He was taken to the hospital. We don't know yet. He was breathing when we got here, so there's a good chance he'll make it."

"Joe tried to warn me. I had no idea Tom was— well—how could I know?" My thoughts bounded in several directions.

If Nicole hadn't gotten sick, we might never have seen her again. I cupped my face in my hands and let the tears fall in earnest.

35
CHAPTER

A week passed. My last recollection was the sight of ten police officers charging into the basement like ants attacking a picnic. At home my furry critters surrounded me. Max clung to my side like a magnet. The Ackermanns supplied me with a month's worth of chicken noodle soup. The media decamped — finally — after a steady round of interviews outside my apartment building.

I spent one night in the hospital, making sure I didn't have a concussion from my chair dive. The doctor said the knife nick on my throat wouldn't leave a scar, but I wasn't so sure about the scars inside my mind. Sleep was my only escape, but the sound of that fatal gunshot woke me up several nights in a row.

The scene in the basement played over and over in my head. Tom was lying in his own blood. He was my friend for so long. Why couldn't I see who he really was? I kept thinking about Jerard's brother's fiancée, Clarissa. What were her last thoughts? How would Jerard and his brother, and her brother Joe, ever get over such a violent death?

I needed to be with my pals and my larger-than-life hero, Jerard, so I invited them over for a casual dinner. I was building a new kind of strength to move forward, and I was no longer going to do it alone.

I pushed off the couch and dismissed all negative thoughts. My body was light—my burdens had been lifted. I wanted to reassure my friends that I was recovering and they were not to worry. The old Sarah would have shoved them away and hidden out. I wasn't that person anymore. In fact, I was going to embrace my friends, especially Jerard. A flame of readiness ignited me.

I shopped at Bruno's Gourmet Deli on Columbus Avenue where I picked up fresh ingredients for my famous pasta primavera, a Cabernet, and Bruno's delicious tiramisu for dessert. I went all out that night and even lit a small fire. I filled my aunt's crystal vase with pink and violet gladiolas. When I set the TV trays with my aunt's china, silver, and cloth napkins, I giggled. *No paper plates tonight.*

The scent of the garlic, basil, and oregano simmering on the stove summoned two wagging tails to my feet. "Okay, you two deserve something special tonight." I retrieved a bowl of small chicken bits and rewarded each dog a piece. I toured my enchanting setting. Tonight this room would be filled with irreplaceable friendship.

At 6:00 p.m. the doorbell rang; I caught my breath and engaged the buzzer. "Who's there?"

"It's us." Paul's reassuring voice filtered through the receiver.

I buzzed them in, unlocked the bolts and swung the door wide so two dogs and a grateful friend could welcome Paul, Liz, Nicole, and Bill. They took off their coats and hung them on the rack.

"Gladiolas. Beautiful." Nicole glided over to the vase and ran her hand over the soft petals.

"Wow, your TV trays have certainly gone upscale. Fine china, sterling, linen napkins. This is a treat." Liz clasped her hands.

We hugged.

Liz asked. "Where's Jerard?"

"He's taking a cab and should be here shortly."

The buzzer sounded again. "It's me." Jerard's easygoing voice charmed me.

His footsteps hit the lobby stairs. He came down the hallway holding flowers. Before I could say hello, he embraced me and planted a long, deep kiss on my lips. The bouquet pressed into my back, releasing the fragrance of roses. My skin flushed. His kiss made me wonder. Should I ask my guests to come back later? The dogs were weaving between our feet. Back to reality. He stepped away from me, bent down, and rubbed Max and Gracey behind their ears.

After a moment Jerard looked past the dogs to our friends who lingered, watching our intimate moment. "I thought I was the first one to arrive," he said.

Nicole flapped her hand. "It's okay, please go on. Don't let us interrupt you. I'd like to see a rerun of that kiss—for pointers. Bill and I need a brush-up lesson." She nudged Bill's side.

My words rushed out. "Okay, the entertainment's over, you guys. Let's eat." I couldn't stop thinking about that kiss. *You don't know it yet, Jerard, but you're spending the night.*

We loaded our plates in the kitchen and then huddled together in the front room, the crackling fire chasing away the foggy chill. Dinner was a huge success—not a crumb left from the tiramisu. I picked up the empty plates and headed to the kitchen.

When I came back into the front room, I collected the remaining silverware. Nicole, Bill, Liz, Paul, and Jerard folded their trays and returned to the couch. Gracey curled up on Liz's lap. Jerard followed me into the kitchen with the last of the glassware.

"I wonder—what's going on in there?" Liz's voice carried into the kitchen.

I said, "I heard that. We're just going to rinse off the dishes." I couldn't help wondering if maybe we could grab another one of those kisses.

Max, my little protector, tailed me back into the kitchen. Ever since I'd arrived home from the hospital, he hadn't let me out of his sight.

A few minutes passed while I stacked the dishes in the

sink. Two arms circled my waist. Surprised, I let my shoulders rise and fall.

Max started his low growl. "I didn't mean to startle you," Jerard murmured in my ear. He backed up enough to kneel and give Max a small head rub. "Sorry, Max."

I dried my hands with the dish towel and turned to face him. "I'm still a little nervous, but I'm working hard to not let it take over me. I killed Tom and that's something I'm going to need help processing. I have an appointment with a counselor next week."

Once again Jerard drew me close. "Good idea. Some things we can't do on our own, and although you saved our lives, you also have to deal with having killed someone. I've experienced it firsthand. You'll get through this." He glided his hands through my hair and smoothed a few strands down to my shoulder. "You have a lot of support."

"I know and believe me, I'm going to accept all the help available. No more trying to do everything on my own; no more shutting people out." I let my head rest on his chest as a hot surge rippled.

Max shifted between our feet, using his tiny body to separate us. His teeth claimed a mouthful of Jerard's lower pant leg.

"Hey, crocodile mouth, *I'm* not the enemy here." Jerard extended a hand for Max to sniff. The dog released the material and offered a small lick of approval.

"Good boy, Max." My voice was soft and reassuring. "He has a possessive side when it comes to me."

"Apparently." Max decided that sitting on Jerard's foot would show who was in control of the situation.

Jerard said, "Okay, I understand completely. Quite fond of her myself."

Max's tail shifted back and forth.

Jerard had just earned some points.

He brushed the side of my head. "The swelling around your ear's gone down."

I winced, ignoring the pain his fingers caused. "Still tender."

"The headaches?" His voice soothed me, and he stroked my shoulders lightly.

"Not as bad." I draped my arms around his neck. "No more words. Show me how concerned you are."

He kissed my forehead, my cheek, and then reeled me into his velvet lips. I welcomed them without hesitation. His hands drifted down, and our hips melded as his kiss went deeper.

I lost all awareness of my surroundings and dove into euphoria. His kiss settled on my neck, and he stopped. Backing away slightly, he smoothed his fingers across the bandage that covered my throat.

"Is it painful?"

"No. I'm going to be okay. Enough about my injuries. How's your wound?" I asked. My vision riveted on the spot where the knife plunged into his side. When I pictured the blood oozing onto his shirt and coat that night, my strength slackened.

His fingers touched the injury. "I'm okay. After everyone leaves you can look at my scar." He tickled my side.

"Did I ever thank you for finding me that night?"

"Yes, you did—only about a hundred times." His lips brushed a kiss on mine.

"Hey, you two!" Nicole's voice broke up any chance for us to continue.

Jerard's Cheshire cat grin told me he hadn't finished romancing me yet. He clasped my hand and we returned to the front room.

36
CHAPTER

Not long afterward my dear friends sat wedged on the couch. While Jerard and I sat on the opposite loveseat, Max nestled between us.

"It's time to go over this whole ugly event, try to put your minds at peace." Jerard said. "You already know I was a lieutenant with the Tampa Police Department. Paul told you about Clarissa, my brother's fiancée."

Bill bent forward. "We've been wondering about the details."

The group's heads shook up and down in agreement.

Jerard hesitated for a moment—tears formed in the corners of his eyes. I squeezed one of his hands while he brushed the moisture away with the other. "Sorry, it's hard to think about it. My brother Mike has a long road ahead of him."

"Why didn't you let me in on this when you first got

to the city?" Paul raised an eyebrow. "I need some answers."

"I couldn't," Jerard said. "I was afraid this guy was going to get away again, and I took care not to release too many details. I really appreciated your support at the end."

Paul scrunched up his face and released a heavy sigh. He rose and offered his hand for a hearty shake. "Glad I could help." He wagged a finger. "But next time you better let me know in advance if you need assistance. Wait—I'd rather not have a next time."

I hoisted Max onto my lap. "How did you figure out it was Tom?" I asked.

"Remember the day I told you I was driving down to Half Moon Bay to check on a client?"

"You mean the day I did my own private investigating, tailing you to art galleries on the square?" I poked his arm.

"Yes. Before I moved to San Francisco, I made it a point to stop at as many coastal galleries as I could. I left my card with the owners and asked them to call me if they had any suspicious customers."

"Did you warn them about the serial killer?" Liz gnawed a fingernail.

"Yeah," he confirmed. "One of the owners from Half Moon Bay did call me back. She'd had an awful feeling about one guy who came into her gallery a few days earlier. She said she was very intuitive, and he'd gotten uncomfortably close to her. He started asking personal questions. Was she married? Was she the owner of the gallery? Then her husband came in and she tried to introduce him to the customer.

"The stranger headed toward the front door and left without acknowledging her husband. She described him as six foot, maybe taller, long red hair, and a beard. He wore a black T-shirt, white shorts, and flip-flops. The guy's blue eyes captured her attention—they were unforgettable."

"Yes, his eyes snared many a woman." The hairs prickled on the back of my neck.

"This lady was not only intuitive, she had the smarts to take the paper cup he used to get a drink of water from the cooler next to her desk. She saved it. *Bingo!* Both DNA and fingerprints. Everything started to fall in place: I had everything I needed, plus the artist's drawing from Karen Johnson, the girl who got away."

"I can't believe we didn't see this side of Tom." Nicole squeezed her eyebrows together.

Liz peered at her. "When you look back, Tom always flirted with you at his restaurant."

"That creeps me out—I could have been his next victim." She hid her eyes behind her hands.

Bill provided Nicole a reassuring hug. "It's okay, honey."

I massaged the side of my head. "I'm still having nightmares. I get up and check my door locks two or three times a night. I think I'm developing some kind of disorder."

Next thing I knew, Nicole crossed the room. She said, "I'll never forgive myself, Sarah, for asking you to take over for me that night." She clasped my hands. "It might be a good idea for you to get some counseling."

"Nicole, you have to let this go or you may need some therapy, too. It wasn't your fault."

"I'll try." She resumed her seat next to Bill.

A sense of calm swept over me. I cruised the faces of my small troop. "Listen, everyone. I came through this with the realization that I'm a fighter. Can you believe what I've accomplished in the last few weeks? I conquered my fear of performing and took out a serial killer. I'm moving forward, thanks to all of you. It'll take some time to heal, but I'm definitely traveling in the right direction." Adrenaline rejuvenated me.

Their silence was unbearable.

"I could use a good nod that you agree."

They delivered a chorus of "yes."

After the merriment died down Jerard offered up some news. "Joe wanted me to let you know he's doing fine. He gets out of the hospital tomorrow and he appreciates all the flowers and cards. What a good guy. He's thankful there can be some closure in his life now that we've found Clarissa's killer."

I sent out a silent thank you. "That's the best news. I'm thankful Joe lived. I wasn't sure he'd make it that night. We'll take him out to dinner when he feels better."

"How about we change the subject? Paul and I have an announcement." Liz swiveled around and smoothed out her skirt. "I'm pregnant." Liz placed her hands on her chest.

I scrambled over and knelt in front of them. "I'm so happy for you."

Bill, Nicole, and Jerard lined up for congratulatory squeezes.

"I guess you noticed I've been a little crabby and short-tempered lately." Liz arched her eyebrows.

Everyone, except for Nicole, chimed in. "No, we didn't notice. What are you saying?"

Nicole waited until the enthusiastic crowd settled. "I certainly picked up on it. No offense, Liz, but you've been a royal pain in the ass." The group waited in silence for a response from Liz.

She wacked Nicole's knee. "One thing I can count on is that you always tell me how you feel. I'm two months along, due in July." She caressed her belly.

"Can you believe I'm going to be a dad?" A twinkle flashed in Paul's eyes.

"Since we're sharing good news," Nicole added, "Bill and I also have an announcement." She edged forward on the cushion. "We're opening our own gallery. Half will display my mosaics and the other half will show Bill's miniature collection of Civil War soldiers."

No one spoke for a few seconds. I wasn't sure about art and the Civil War co-starring in the same gallery. But, then again, Bill and Nicole proved that opposites attract. Maybe these diverse displays would attract an interesting clientele.

"A little strange, but we'll see where it goes." Bill rubbed his hands together.

Paul perked up, shifting back to a more serious

conversation. "Hey, Jerard, what are your plans? You going to stick around for a while, or do you have to go back to Tampa?"

Jerard's fingers guided my face toward his and those emerald eyes surfaced. He said, "I plan to stick around for a while. I'm actually thinking about going back on the police force, so maybe I'll apply here in San Francisco. Tired of moving around so much. In the meantime I've signed us all up for another swing class." Jerard examined the group—they grimaced. "I'm kidding." He said. The number of exhales could have put the flames out in my fireplace.

The next thing I heard was the group hooting with relief, including me.

I set Max back on the floor and got another glimpse of that nasty scar on Jerard's hand. "You never did tell us how you got that wound. I want details this time, no joking around. Give us, the truth, Mister." I tried on an overblown serious expression.

Jerard produced a wide grin. "I wish I could tell you it was while I was trying to catch some bad guys, or that I was hired by a wife who suspected her husband was cheating and he ended up slicing me."

"No fantasies—just the facts." I swatted the air.

"At the time I was taking a furniture-making class to relax my nerves and take my mind off the case. I wasn't paying attention and I got into a squabble with the electric saw. The saw won and that's the truth. Eagle Scout's honor." He crinkled his forehead.

I tousled his hair. "Guess that could be the truth. That is, if Jerard *is* your real name."

EPILOGUE

March 2015

I'm backstage at Lorraine's One and Only Jazz Club—
my opening night. I finger the curtain slightly to the side
and have a direct observation of the table filled with my
friends. These pals are like family to me. I signed a one-
year contract with Lorraine. Tom's restaurant, Courtney's, closed, and I doubt they'll ever find a new buyer.

The lights dim and I roll my shoulders a couple of
times. *No more saying I can't do this; you're doing it, girl!* I
squint at Nicole and Liz who huddle in conversation
that involves quite a bit of hilarity. The guys clink their
glasses, making a toast of some sort.

There's Joe joining the group and a striking young
woman is holding his hand. What a surprise. Nicole
managed to set up a blind date again. She told me she

had the perfect girl for Joe. My little matchmaker. She didn't do too badly with Jerard.

Luckily, Joe recovered nicely from his stab wound. No major organs were damaged. Was he going to stay in San Francisco or go back home to Tampa? The lovely lady next to him might make that decision for him.

Jerard's been coaxing him into applying to the San Francisco Police Department since Joe helped a lot with this case and has good instincts. Joe told him he'll give it some thought.

Liz and Paul are going to have twins, a boy and a girl. Lately a desire to have children has been on my mind. I've pictured Jerard and I guiding a stroller along Fisherman's Wharf. Nicole and Bill's Art and Civil War Gallery has done amazingly well. The mix of the two themes has brought a sizable crowd through their doors every weekend. Their marriage is so unique. The way they continue to show their affection for each other gives you the impression they just started dating. I couldn't ask for a better group of friends. They've given me the gift of love, loyalty, and humor. They never once left me stranded.

Jerard's brother Mike is sitting next to him. Once Tom's murder case closed, Mike came out to San Francisco to spend time with him. He finally had some closure after Clarissa's death and has even given some thought to dating.

Jerard applied for a position in the San Francisco Police Department—what a surprise. He's had enough traveling and wants to settle. Paul's been a great help, introducing him to the officers at the precinct and helping him study for upcoming exams. They've developed a solid friendship.

Jerard and I are taking it slow, getting to know each other without all the drama. When we make love, the world disappears. When his arms are around me, I have a sense of belonging. If there were any man I'd trust with my life, it would be him. He's the one I always hoped to find—passionate, a great listener, kind, and patient. He and I are no longer on the outskirts of love—we're smack in the middle. Wait a minute—he's no longer at the table. Where'd he go? I'm ready to perform. My chest tightens.

Lorraine welcomes the audience. I smooth out my dress, flip my hair off my shoulders, and let curls cascade down my back. Jerard hasn't returned to his seat. Someone's hand strokes the back of my neck. I let go of the curtain, turn around, and run smack into him.

"I wanted to come backstage and have a moment with you." His lips tease mine, so lightly at first, then deeper. The thirst I have for him almost makes me forget I'm about to go onstage.

I take a small step away. "We'd better stop now, or I may just have to take you back to my dressing room. I'm glad you came backstage."

"I love you, Sarah." For a moment he holds my face in his hands.

I lace my fingers through his. "I know deep in my soul I can trust you with all the love I'm willing to hand over."

Jerard heads back to the table.

Lorraine takes the microphone and announces, "Here she is, Sarah Soon." Those words sweep me into a future I'd never before thought possible.

I take a deep breath and air fills my lungs. I step forward onstage and embrace the spotlight.

ACKNOWLEDGMENTS

I would like to thank my late husband, Norman D. Taylor, who gave me courage. It was a challenge for me to open my computer every morning for almost five years and work on creating this book. My husband was a true teacher in my life and encouraged me to try different things, not to be afraid to fall flat on my face once in a while. It's taken a great deal of courage to write, but the experience has given me so many gifts in return.

Many thanks to James T. Torian, my dad, who gave me my sense of humor. It helps to laugh when you're trying to figure out how to knock someone off in your book. My dad was a true entertainer. I inherited that trait from him, so I incorporate humor in my writing.

Kudos to my aunt Sheila Radford and her daughter Tammy Aguiar, who are my computer gurus. Without their constant help and reassurance, my computer would have been tossed out onto Highway 99 and crunched by snow tires.

Thank you to my beautiful stepdaughter, Stacey Taylor, retired Lieutenant, Orange County Sheriff's Department, and Chief of Police, Rancho Santa Margarita, California. She helped me develop the logistics of the basement scene and gave me other crime scene information.

Thanks go to Bethany King and Pamela Marino, who have been my life-long friends and cheerleaders throughout this journey. Thank you for letting me share my mini-size breakdowns, my tears, and my joys.

I have to mention the little soul mates that have kept me company all these years, my two dachshunds, Roxy and Zack. They give me unconditional love and all they ask of me is a constant supply of snacks.

A great deal of gratitude goes to Gini Grossenbacher, my editor, teacher, and dear friend. When Gini suggested I take my two-page flash fiction and turn it into a novella, I immediately wanted to run and do something productive, like clean out my purse or put together that two-thousand-piece puzzle. Without Gini's inspiration, I would not have completed this incredible adventure and believe me, I had to wear a pith helmet quite often to wander in and out of this jungle.

My main support group has been Elk Grove Writers and Artists. We have been sitting together in Gini's living room on Tuesday nights, writing and sharing, since 2013. You are the women who have given me strength when I wanted to give up. Each and every one of you are the soul of this book: Lorna Norisse, Liz Abess, Lisa Dornback, Evangeline Freathy, Sandra Heaton, Judy Vaughan, Amanda Williams, Christine Templeton, Loy Holder, Kris Schoeller, and Lorna Rae Warrington.

I also wish to thank my EGWA manuscript group. Well, this was an experience. I entered the room with the first thirty pages of my manuscript thinking, "What am I doing here?" Their guidance taught me to look at each line, show don't tell, go deeper. They gave me the confidence to move forward to that last page. Many thanks to those who worked on my novella: Robert Pacholik, Judy Vaughan, Margaret Duarte, Elaine Faber, Susan Harrison, Rick Davis, Sharon Darrow, and Lorna Norisse.

A special thank you to Karen Phillips, graphic designer for the cover of my book; JGKS Press, the publishing company; Patricia Foulk and Lisa Dornback, the proofreaders; Maureen Cutajar from Go Published, the interior designer; and Cristina Deptula, from Authors Large and Small, the publicist. Without these wonderful people, I would never have been able to send my book out into the world.

ABOUT THE AUTHOR

Kathleen Taylor earned a Bachelor of Arts degree in Drama and Dance from the University of the Pacific in Stockton, California. She is a retired professional dancer, choreographer, and teacher, with a strong background in musical theatre. She toured with the New Dance Company of New Zealand for one year. She was co-founder of New Dance Company in Stockton, California. Not only did she teach modern and jazz dance at the University of the Pacific, she was also guest teacher at the Idyllwild Summer Arts program, located in in the San Jacinto Mountains of Riverside County, California. She received the Outstanding Achievement Award in Dance from the Stockton Arts Commission and was granted the California State Legislature Certificate of Recognition.

The author joined Gini Grossenbacher's Elk Grove Writers & Artists in 2013. This book arose out of a two-page flash fiction story, and with Gini's encouragement and expertise, those two pages turned into *Death By Arrangement,* the author's first novella.

Kathleen Torian Taylor is also a working poet. Four of her poems have been published in the 2020 Redwood Writers anthology, *And Yet.* Her poems have appeared in *The Haight Ashbury Literary Journal.* She received honorable mention for her poem, "If You're Looking for Perfections," from 1997's Soul-Making Keats Literary Competition in San Francisco where she read her work in a poetry invitational at the San Francisco Public Library.

For further information, please contact the author:

Website: *www.kathleentoriantaylor.com*
Facebook: *www.facebook.com/kathleen.taylor.50364592*
Twitter: *twitter.com/KathleenTorian*
Instagram: *www.instagram.com/kathleentortay*